ENTROPIC

STORIES

# ENTROPIC

*R.W. Gray*

NeWest Press

Library and Archives Canada Cataloguing in Publication

Gray, R.W. (Robert William), 1969–, author
Entropic / R.W. Gray.

Issued in print and electronic formats. ISBN 978-1-927063-86-6 (pbk.). — ISBN 978-1-927063-87-3 (epub). — ISBN 978-1-927063-88-0 (mobi)

I. Title.

PS8613.R389E67 2015          C813'.6          C2014-906489-6
                                               C2014-906490-X


Editor: Suzette Mayr
Book design: Natalie Olsen, Kisscut Design
Cover photo © michaket / photocase.com
Author photo: Reuben Stewart

Canada Council for the Arts    Conseil des Arts du Canada    Canadian Heritage    Patrimoine canadien
accessCOPYRIGHT FOUNDATION    Alberta Government    Edmonton    edmonton arts council

NeWest Press acknowledges the support of the Canada Council for the Arts, the Alberta Foundation for the Arts, and the Edmonton Arts Council for support of our publishing program. We acknowledge the financial support of the Government of Canada through the Canada Book Fund for our publishing activities.

#201, 8540 – 109 Street
Edmonton, Alberta  T6G 1E6
780.432.9427
NeWest Press    www.newestpress.com

*No bison were harmed in the making of this book.*

Printed and bound in Canada    1 2 3 4 5 17 16 15

*for A.*
*for the days of reckoning*

# CONTENTS

BLINK

*"Look for the woman in the dress.*
*If there is no woman, there is no dress."*

— COCO CHANEL

# BLINK

**YOU'D UNDERSTAND IF** you could see her. Here, in the Saturday morning street market, a black coffee in one hand, the other gently running over the spines of tattered books on a book table. Everything about her conspires toward composure. Each strand of hair flowing with the others, the perfectly cut line where her hairline parts. She's not a woman who fidgets. She has the composure of the stone women who hold up temple roofs.

Do the melancholy candle vendor, the grim Belgian chocolatier, the slow grazing market goers feel this way around her? Redundant. Untethered, wanting to hold her hand so as to not float away.

Lost. I've lost sight of her.

The market air shudders. Oceans lie down on me. A flock of wingless, cawless birds fling themselves over the buildings, the Saturday shoppers motionless, paper thin and oblivious. Lost.

She turns then and I see her in profile, eating caramelized ginger delicately from a paper bag like it's a secret between her and the ginger. Not lost.

Silly. I think, silly. Like a child. My mother must have used this word once. Many times. Don't be silly.

I mention this to my therapist, how I lose her. It's not the first time. He, predictably, asks how it makes me feel. Silly, I say. He, predictably, looks concerned.

I don't tell him how I am braced for this pain now, braced waiting for the next sinkhole, for the sound to suck out of the room, and the deep, sea-floor silence to press in.

She'll turn then, colour gushing back in, and see my furrowed forehead, throw me a subtle lift of her eyebrows to ask what's up, as if nothing. Silly.

Back at our apartment, in the moment before I throw my keys on the hall table I look out over the catalogue-photo-ready living room, the sofa, the cushions, the blinds, and see the apartment is a reflection of her; I am redundant even here. How long would I have to be gone, out of these rooms, out in the streets with the other strangers before she would forget me entirely. She might find one of my baseball caps in the closet, my slippers on the bathroom floor, and wonder where they came from or who they belonged to. A guest from her last birthday party maybe. A small mystery that would leave her only slightly uneasy.

I am no different from anyone else though. No one could make her turn and see them more than I do. If she's going to forget someone, why not me?

She stands in the kitchen doorway resting on one leg, crisply eating sugar snap peas, smiling wider to say hello. Lost. Cut from the air, the room suddenly musty, dust motes hanging where her breath was a moment ago.

Maybe, I say to my therapist, maybe I am afraid. Maybe the silence is my fear she'll leave.

The therapist nods, slow and deliberate, like he knew I would say this.

"And you've had your hearing checked?"

This question makes me pause. I was willing to concede that I was imagining her there and then gone, the lost time, that it was just my anxious mind. A therapist resorting to literal, physical possibilities rather than all the possible figurative ones makes me pause.

"Yes," I lie.

She calls out from the kitchen, "Honey you're home!" as I put my keys on the hall table. I find her there and kiss her on the back of her neck as she cuts carrots. We ask about our days.

After dinner, I watch the news on a couch full of too many pillows, peripherally aware of the clink of her stacking dishes in the kitchen, running water in the bathroom sink, opening and closing the bureau drawers in the bedroom, then the fridge opening in the kitchen. A local news story reports that a dog tried to swim across the river and got stuck on a sandbar where he's been waiting to be rescued for they suspect a week, boating on the river at a minimum due to the rains. The rescued dog looks happy but skeletal.

I want a snack and expect to find her in the kitchen but she's not. Room by room I look for her, but I am alone in the apartment. I stand in the middle of the living room caught between two breaths. Like wondering why the key doesn't fit, then realizing you're at the apartment door one floor directly below yours and the horror, even if it's a mistake and for only a moment, the horror of being shut out of one's own life.

Like the sea floor falling away.

"What?" she asks in the kitchen doorway, drying her hands on an orange tea towel.

"I couldn't find you."

"I was right here."

"Were you in the bedroom?"

"No."

She turns away from me as she moves her hair behind her ear. A rare gesture, it plays out for me in slow motion and then a montage of all the other times I have seen it: a first date when we went to a pottery class and the room seemed full of fragile, the confusing responsibility of grilling her own food at the Korean restaurant the first time, the moment last summer before leaping off the stone bridge, a dare. She turns away so I won't notice.

I turn and slump down on the couch to watch the last of the news, edgy, upset she might be noticing how weird I've been acting. I notice the silence.

Kitchen, bathroom, bedroom stare back at me from the same catalogue as the living room, photos without her.

First I think she's out at the store. Milk, or crackers maybe. She likes crackers. And milk. Maybe she's angry. She could have said something and I was just not listening again, content to let her carry on conversations without me. But she's missing so I can't ask her. I get the idea she might have left me. As I rush from room to room they feel empty, not waiting for her any longer.

I carefully open her drawers in the bedroom. Underwear discreetly folded, a nest of black bras, balls of socks. No hastily packed suitcases like in the movies.

I notice then that the wardrobe has been moved, the scratches where the legs have been dragged along the floor. Judging by the gouges, it's been moved many times. I wonder why I haven't noticed. I lean my shoulder into it, shudder it along its familiar grooves, revealing behind it a large hole, from knee height and as tall as me. The sudden silence, her absence, the air sucking out of the room, the vertigo and missed steps. A hole in the wall. I step towards the hole, but it looks too small to pass. I shoulder my torso in, then step up and over into the darkness on the other side. These moments in our lives are rare and brutal.

My eyes struggle to adjust to the wall of sharp darkness. I could plummet into an abyss on my next step but the possibility that in the darkness is an explanation breathes beastly on the nape of my neck. I can imagine reading about this in a book or seeing it in a movie. I would shout at the screen not to go into the hole. I would know something awful was going to happen to that man, to me. But I would secretly wish him into the hole. There's no version of this story where the man in the movie just moves the wardrobe back, pretends he never found a hole. He can't just go for coffee or brush his teeth or nap on the living room couch. I stepped through a gap into this hole and now each moment of my existence, this entire life, has shrunk down to these tiny gasping breaths in the dark on the edge of what will happen next.

I crouch, take another step into the darkness, the floor smooth and wooden, my hands moving in front of me in the darkness wanting and afraid to find purchase. Children are usually the ones foolish or desperate enough to go down holes in stories. Maybe I'm scared.

There. Shapes. The floor. The slats of the hardwood. I gently step forward and a blue-ish light bleeds from around the corner up ahead. This might be worse than the darkness. I step forward again. There, on the other side, a room. Just a room. Nothing magical, no rabbits, no hidden worlds. A simple hidden room, maybe once an office or a walk-in closet. I realize now I should have noticed it, guessed the gap between these two rooms was unaccounted-for space. My mind deleted the gap.

She's drawn her legs up under her, her shoulder and head rest to the side of a large desk chair. She sleeps.

Shaking my head, thin film of anger. She had insisted we rent this apartment even though it meant I wouldn't have an office or den of my own. All this time she kept this space to herself.

She sleeps but her face grimaces serious, bothered. Not pretty, she lacks her usual composure. I've never seen this look on her face.

Piled around her feet, an unruly sea of film stock. On the wall above her, a mural of photographs, all of her. Photos of her from every angle, some with notes. "Bad side." "Jaw disappears when head lowered." "Eyes like a penguin." Photos of her sleeping, showering, eating, a whole small collage of her sneezing, coughing, yawning, black felt pen crossing them all out. Dozens and dozens of eliminated faces, a stadium crowd of wasted expressions.

I realize I have never seen her sneeze, cough or even yawn. The photos glow in the half-light of the photo boxes and the idle play of the computer's screen saver. I feel a small happiness. Then it falls. How did I never wonder?

In the blue light I see my hands are shaking. Shock I guess. On the table in front of her, the masses of film stock curling around the room in dark waves. I reach down and lift one strand, hold it up to the light box above her desk. Us, having breakfast, eating omelets. I look angry. We never had this breakfast. Not that I remember. Why was I angry? It seems familiar. Possible.

She stirs. Her eyes open. She starts and stumbles as she tries to stand. I don't move to help her out. She trembles, steadies herself with one hand on the desk, her mouth drawing down in one corner. Terror looks like a seizure on her and I barely recognize her. Another never-seen expression. I add it to the list with the sneezes.

She's speechless. Maybe she's waiting for me to say something, a slight crouch to her stance, wide-eyed like she might run, but the only exit is the hole behind me.

"I don't understand," I hear myself say.


**A WOMAN WITH BRICK DUST** on her hands is a lovely thing. Unexpected, though, of course. She agreed to brick up the hole, the room, the cutting machine and the light boxes, and she agreed not to cut our life into any more pieces.

But first she tried to claw her way out, the truth catching her in a leg trap.

"You're to blame too."

"How long?" I refuse her taunt. "How long have you been doing this?" She shakes her head looking down at her feet, her hair falling loose and over her face. "Since we moved in together?" I don't think she's breathing. "Since we met?" She looks sideways, shoulders cinching up. "So the entire time I've known you."

"I didn't mean to —"

"You what? Didn't mean to? This isn't a slip. This isn't 'Oh I forgot to get toilet paper.' There's an editing suite behind the walls of our bedroom."

She scrutinizes her hands clasped tightly in front of her. I think she's crying. I've never seen her cry and now I've seen it twice in one day.

"You're not innocent in this," she says, eyes looking to cut me from this moment "If you weren't such a perfectionist."

"That's rich."

"I knew when I met you. The way you comb your hair, your apartment, everything is just so. I thought you were gay."

"Maybe I am. Maybe you edited it out," I slap back.

She stumbles. Can't help herself. Looks right, hand to mouth to cover the rays of a smile.

I turn away, too, concealing my slip of a smile. Her shoulders shaking, over her shoulder I see her pained laughter. I cover my face with my hands, shaking now too. The anger falls from the room as the air floods back in.

"Do we do this a lot?" I ask.

"What? Fight?"

I nod.

She shrugs. "I don't know. I guess. I don't know how much other people fight."

We sit in the living room side by side on the couch and despite all the furniture and throw pillows and pictures she's chosen for us, the room feels blank, as though we are just about to move in.

And in the days that follow, she really moves in. I can't honestly say I love it all, the various and sundry things that flow back in now that she's stopped editing. I even vaguely resent her. For now I know she could elide these moments if I asked her to. She's made it this way. Even breakfast is not just breakfast anymore: each morning now, the small noise she makes to clear her throat when she's eating cereal. I think she might be lactose intolerant. See, this is what I learn now. Moment to moment another surprise arrives. She sometimes sneaks a cigarette out on the fire escape; snaps at me whenever I leave my underwear on the bathroom floor because apparently I have been leaving my underwear on the bathroom floor for god knows how long; her face before she sneezes is a hideous thing to behold and she sneezes all the time; she farts on the toilet and also doesn't seem to know the bathroom door also closes. I perpetually wait for the next flaw to show up, flinching with a sort of relationship version of shell shock.

I guess with other people I've loved, the flaws show themselves subtly over time. With her, all these flaws arrived at once. I'm just saying it's a lot to process. Maybe with time.

I imagine the cut, the tearing. I imagine potential edits she might make later, though she has promised she won't. But the possibility haunts us now. Was breakfast worse than I know? Was there some angry row between us, me sick of her throat clearing, sick of the way she eats cereal? Her sick of my inability to fold a newspaper back to its original form, my tattered and depressed housecoat, or the way I tilt to one side and fart at the table thinking she doesn't know. Maybe the crotch and pit morning smell of me, my compost bin morning breath. I can never know for sure. The past will always be unreliable now.

"What?" she asks the table resentfully.

"Nothing."

"Obviously it's something. Otherwise you wouldn't be looking at me like that."

It still startles me to see her brow wrinkle up, her eyes glare. These little contortions of her face, though not pretty, do offer some consolation: when you've been in love with a perfectly composed woman, the imperfections Velcro her to you. As the flaws accumulate, I take it as a challenge: I must love her. And at the same time, now it feels like she might actually need me, because not everyone could love all this.

Editing, it turns out, is an invisible business. We all do it. Blink and you've edited. People in movie theatres, hiding from what's scary hold up their hands and hide. A surprising number of pedestrians cover their eyes just before cars hit them. She just found ways to close our eyes during the unpleasant parts. I'd have to say that she was the best possible teacher. As untrustworthy as the past might be, she made it a fine example of good editing. To fashion the garment with no visible seams. She showed me how. I had the means, I just needed the motivation and it came soon enough.

A small moment. A romantic overture turned bad. I took flowers to her work. Sure, I felt things had gotten more real between us, but my old anxieties that she would always leave were now replaced by not knowing if each moment was real and unedited. I was second-guessing us. So I took the flowers to her work and they were flowers to make things okay between us, maybe even more real. When I got to the gallery where she worked, she was out and the receptionist didn't know where. All the fears I'd hoped to cover up with the flowers were there then. Had she gone back to our place to edit some offense, some flaw, or worse, was she seeing someone else behind my back, someone she could edit without them even knowing? The flowers, irises and lilies, glared up at me cloying and needy. I dropped them in the silver garbage can near the entrance and left without saying anything to the receptionist.

On the street outside I see her, a coffee in her hand, the gallery's owner laughing at something she said. I turn and see through the gallery glass the receptionist watching, enthralled to see what might happen next. I turn back, think to flee, but she sees me mid-smile, mid sip of her latte. I turn and cross the street in a rush, though I can still hear the gallery owner's voice "Isn't that —" before the traffic noise and distance swallow their words.

Walking home with my skinless face and boneless hands, in the passing windows I could catch glimpses of what I was becoming. This truth was shallow, flawed, and less real than all her careful fictions. I could see so clearly what to do. I rushed back to the apartment, took the hammer and chisel out of the hall closet and smashed the mortar away from the bricks, arduous work, my t-shirt sopping around the neck, blisters bubbling in the crook between my thumbs and forefingers. Brick by brick I broke into the darkness beyond, the mortar thankfully still loose and wet in spots. The room glowed in the same blue light, waiting for me: the cutting machine, the light boxes, the piles of unused footage waiting like casualties.

I cleanly fix the morning. Rewind to the moment before I enter the gallery, the morning light glancing off the glass door, my hand reaches for the handle, my reflection before me, the flowers in my other hand and I pause the moment so it hangs there, my hand inches from the door handle. Cut. I don't enter the gallery, there are no flowers, and I don't try to play the good boyfriend and then devolve into an insecure and angry mess. On her way back from coffee she does not see me flee, does not find the bewildered receptionist and the discarded flowers. The frame before the cut hangs in my mind: the blue irises still closed, paintbrushes waiting. Life spills in to fill the gaps. In the entranceway of the gallery, she shakes her head, a wonky smile to cover her unease, and then she strides back to her desk and the sleeping computer screen.

When she walks in the door later that night, she's surprised by flowers on the hall table. She forgets any gaps she sensed in the morning. Editing gave me this second chance. Any guilt, any conflicted feelings I felt about tearing down the bricks dissolve when I see the tear-edged smile as she stands in the hallway still in her coat. I get it now. Know what made her do it, and what made her keep on doing it.

I don't brick the wall back up. But neither do I abuse the power. I leave the wardrobe undisturbed in front of the hole for weeks. The ruts in the floor look the same. She'll never know, I think.

But then I find myself splicing, cutting, taping the film pieces together to cover the gaps I leave in our lives more than I'd probably like. Truth be told, yes, that little cough is gone. She no longer appears lactose intolerant, no longer coughs incessantly after ice cream or strains her neck to belch like a cat struggling with a hairball after Brie. But I'm not a butcher. Her cold feet still alarm mine moments after we turn out the bedside lamps, she still laughs like a sneeze, and when she's thirsty her breath still smells like a beach abandoned by the sea. I only thin out the difficulties, don't remove them.

I can't be sure she doesn't still sneak in there, too, abbreviate little jagged pieces of our breakfasts, our grocery aisle scuffles. Thing is, I care a little less now. There's a remnant beauty in these yawnless, coughless, slurpless breakfasts. These nothing moments look a lot like happiness.

Then, late morning, she's out the door with a travel mug of coffee and a piece of butterless toast between her teeth, late for her bus, and I Sisyphus the wardrobe aside and shuffle into the hidden room with a fresh cup of coffee and a handful of worry. As breakfasts go, we had had better mornings. Everything I did irritated her: brewed the coffee too weak, made too much noise with my spoon against the cereal bowl, slurped the dregs of milk, laughed at the newspaper comics. At the last one I looked up, hoping she'd ask what was funny so I could share it with her, but her expression, the small dimple between her eyebrows, her narrowed eyes, confused me: a little like hatred and a little like the desire for me to cease existing. The least I can do is cut out the breakfast table, edit it so she thinks I got up from bed and sleepily fumbled myself straight to the gym. Give her a quiet morning so she never has to wear that face.

Slice of the blade between the frames, then I tape together an easy enough edit. Remove the breakfast scene. She'd already scraped out the last of a non-fat yogurt and licked the spoon clean, and gulped two cups of tea anyway. And remove my gym bag and me. She will assume the rest. I teeter on the edge of the cut, a little shiver as I feel how each cut pushes me closer to the precipice — how it feels to remove myself from her life to make her happier.

She clears her throat. But the image on the screen is paused. I squint confused by this glitch, then a jolt of realization seizes my muscles. She's standing behind me in the editing room. I turn, the train of muscles in my neck fighting not to see. In shock. "I just —" But I see then she's not angry. Her face looks weary. Sad.

"Now you know," she says.

We walk. Back and forth across the bridge that spans the water between here and the north side of the city, cross over the narrows, down to the entrance where two lions stand guard, then we refuse to pass, turning back, crossing again to the other side where two more lions stand in wait, never leaving the bridge.

We are up in the air. We are in between. We pace this way. A conversation we both promise not to edit now or later. As we discuss whether we can continue this way, unedited, uncensored with this graphic kind of love. Can we handle it?

Freighters pass freely below this bridge. Jumpers who jump don't survive. The lions stand guard over each side of the span, this grand arch of a kingdom in between, certainty below and beyond its gates.

Would we have reached this conversation sooner if we had never edited at all? We reach the lions, turn back again, as we decide whether we love the idea of our relationship more than the real footage. Her head is lowered, watching my feet when I speak, watching her own when she speaks. I'm looking up at the blue sea above, scrunching up my eyes, wincing as I try to concentrate and listen. We've never had a conversation this long. A clumsy, wrongly worded, repetitive, regrettable, skinless, honest, and erroneous blather of all the stuff we might have edited out given half a chance and a moment alone. But we have no chances left.

We pace up to the rear haunches of the lions again, the trees rising up flanking the bridge, the currents of the narrows behind us. Dangerously close to the ground now, we hang in this air. No visible cuts. The unending shot. I don't squint. She looks up from our feet, eyes fixed on my clavicles. We have crossed back and forth until all the words are gone and now must experience this moment. To see one another. And so we do.

ENTROPIC

# ENTROPIC

**I RECEIVE THE EMAIL** on a Tuesday night, read it as the rain gusts against the window in splatters. I will remember later what night of the week it is because the contents are too strange for a Tuesday. I am brushing my teeth, aimlessly pacing, when I notice the new message on the computer screen. It's from M. An email sent to a long list of people. I read the message twice. I stride to the sink, rinse my mouth at the tap, decant a glass of water from the jug on the counter, and return to the computer screen braced to read the message again. It doesn't make sense.

I hesitate to call M. I know I won't be the only one calling to ask what the email means. But then I do call. Because I am one of the few he might explain himself to. And I fear how sometimes quiet signs mean terrible things.

I call. We meet for coffee an hour later, the café he usually prefers with the kookaburra on the sign. Their espresso tastes bitter, but he must choose it because the family that runs it is so friendly. I order a latte despite the late hour but I already forfeited sleep the second I read the email.

"So," I say, words in my mind like marbles scattering on a tile floor. I shift in my seat, look away to glance back at him. My mother told me never to look at welding sparks or I could go blind. At school they told us not to look directly at the eclipse and we built devices out of cardboard and mirrors so we could still see it indirectly. His beauty is unmanageable.

The waitress forgets his shot of espresso twice, returning with a blush each time to apologize, has to return for a fourth trip with the cinnamon he asked for, returns twice to wipe down the table, and another time to restock the sugars. At the next table, two men take turns cataloging all M's parts, tatters of a hushed conversation between them. They think they are being discreet.

He comments on the rain, gesturing to wipe it off where it has soaked his thighs and around the neck of his shirt. I nod, make busy with sipping my latte, nod some more, bracing through the small pains of being so close to his beauty. Today, his mouth. He has the perfect mouth. Not too big, not too little, lips proportionate without an overly determined upper lip or an overly pouty bottom. These details mere footnotes to a singular thought, that he has a mouth that must taste like —

"You're wondering . . ." he opens.

"Yeah. I guess I am."

"What it's about or why I invited you?"

"I guess both."

"I've invited you because I need your help."

"I'm not sure . . . I don't see how I can help."

He explains then why. How perhaps it might be hard for me to see because although I am attractive, I am not beautiful like him.

A twinge of hurt, but hurt for the lie, not the truth of what he says. To be next to him is to be a void next to great flares of a blue star. Like him is not an option.

His is the kind of beauty people abandon themselves for. Maybe just in pieces, but sometimes whole. His beauty the gravity well.

He tries to explain. How beauty feels in the eyes of all the beholders. Strangers passing on sidewalks gaze up the length of him, in cafés and grocery stores they caress his back, his forearms, press into him on buses, the sighs of women inhaling against him on the subway and in elevators. A woman in a lineup at the drug store gestured for him to lean down so she could whisper something and then bit his earlobe and drew blood. A stranger at the reception desk at his work asked to see his abdominal muscles. A man in the showers at the gym, head down, bear-hugged his naked midriff, crushing the breath from him and didn't release until M called for help. How in a muddy field mud gathers mud, he collapses at the end of his day, a golem burdened into being by the longings of others, crushing what remains of M.

How he has learned to recognize that slight glaze in people's eyes, a gesture towards listening, which is not the same as listening.

I nod. I try to remember what it was like to kiss that mouth. I try to forget.

"It becomes such a responsibility," he explains. When people begin with his beauty, anything he says or does disappoints. The sinkhole in his gut as he sees people reassess, their expression dropping slightly as they focus, see he's not his beauty, glimpse a flaw or worse, something plain just underneath.

For a time at college he found himself saying little. It was an easier time for everyone, he says, but like being anchored to the seabed, reaching hands only two feet below the surface, tethered from the air. He says this, the part about the drowning, and I try to get it to stick in my head, to really listen to that.

"Truly," he uses that word, that word, "truly." "I am exhausted," he says. "I got home last night, got through the door and it felt like I inhaled for the first time all day. Then I looked up and there was a guy in the building across the way with a telescope. I laid in the bathtub, door locked, clothes on for hours."

His eyes pool blue and glassy, a tear runs down one cheek and he brushes it away. I resent him, his beautiful sadness, the ugly crier that I am.

I will help him. He knew this before he hit send. I had a crush on him before anything else. We became friends, of course. But a residue clings. Not like the possibility of anything, but like a slight charge in the air.

In the email, he identified a Saturday a few weeks away. He tells me he feels the wait will let people anticipate it. He has rented a warehouse on the east side, the industrial district, a place where they won't be bothered on a weekend. The email included the address and instructions. Each person is to RSVP to schedule a time. After that, the schedule will be strict. Each person has forty minutes. All told it might take the whole weekend.

"Will you?" he asks.

"What?"

"Will you be the one who takes care of me?"

I feel terrified. Privileged. I am not just one of the others. He has asked me to be there for him.

"I think . . . I think I have to think about it," I say, my breath hitching in my ribs. The two men at the next table, though, look ready to volunteer for anything M might suggest.

Later, I lie in bed, the blank ceiling bored with me. I wind the blankets around my legs, feet suffocate so I throw off the duvet, open the window to the collisions of raindrops on leaves and concrete, lie bare to the wet air breathing into the room, torque the blankets around me until I overheat. Tear them off, relief in the cold salt air, and begin again.

My alarm blares and I have no permissible evidence of sleep. I text him right away, fearful he might have gotten someone else. He messages back. "I didn't ask anyone else. I hoped you would reconsider."

Over the weeks leading up to the day, he forwards me the messages he receives. First some hurried and demanding bookings for time. A few messages offering numbers for crisis lines

and counselors, even a minister. Some use words like "immoral"
and "depraved" and even "pathetic." Then, inevitably, the judg-
mental and concerned ones write back asking for a place in
line. He will not refuse anyone. Time will mean nothing to him
anyway.

I reconsider. I am not sure I can do this. I call him.

"I understand," he says. "It must seem monstrous to you."

I do not know what to say to this. Yes, it does.

"Can I ask you, are you your plainness?" This slips in the
gap between my ribs. "I know you're not. So you see. I'm not
my beauty. I figured this out late, I know. In genetic testing we
remove each gene then let the creature grow to see what the
absence creates. This is all I am suggesting. And I need your help."

I can't refuse him.

The day before, I pick up the supplies he listed on a small
yellow Post-it note. I find a medical supply shop near my work. I
work down the list, dropping things into the basket. He ordered
some of the stuff off the internet already. But as I slide the basket onto the counter I worry the cashier is putting the clues
together, deducing my depravity. He scans item after item,
dropping them into the bag, chatting with the cashier behind
him about a reality show, or maybe a family reunion. Maybe
this kind of thing happens all the time.

I spend the night practicing inserting the needle into an
orange. Then I pierce apples. I compare them to the texture of the
flesh on my arm and wonder which fruit would be more like me.
He is much more muscular than me, everywhere, and I wonder
what kind of fruit his flesh will be. Apples and oranges.

Friday morning, I meet him at the warehouse space early.
That week he hired cleaners from the north shore, three women
in matching uniforms, who stood at the large sliding door to
the warehouse, set their caddies of supplies down, and regarded

the space with indecipherable, grim expressions. He explained how exacting he is to them. He added that he was paying them twice their rate but for that he expected he would not have to ask them to go over any spot again. One of them nodded. He didn't have to ask.

He hired a painting company that specialized in large corporate jobs, made sure they had the ladder and special extensions to reach the ceilings. The next morning, in the thin and merciless morning light he saw where they had left gaps and splotches. He demanded they come back and paint all over again, the resulting white more white than white ever hoped to be.

In the thin, early light glancing off the white space, his eyes spend a lot of time being blue. They aren't blue like water or the sky, or even blue like sapphires. They aren't cold blue or dark like black and betray no hint of green at all. We were half-naked together once. A walk after a dinner, he admitted that most people he met pushed breathlessly to be naked with him, but he didn't feel that with me. Like a man scrambling and failing to hold water in his hands, I knew this trust meant I could get closer to him and, more fatally, that he considered me a friend now. This affection for me meant I could be pathetic with him. So I told him I was okay being single, but I missed the intimacy, the cuddling. Then back at my place, a shirtless, nuzzling, thick pawed short time. Over and over I kept wondering if this might happen again, if maybe we would date, my kisses only half listening.

I think none of this now. His eyes brace me against the wall.

We spread white canvas drop sheets out across the floor. Blue or orange plastic tarps would seem too industrial he decided, especially against the pervasive white paint. I notice this is not just any warehouse. It used to be a sound stage. It is insulated. He must have chosen it for this. A few windows up high he's covered with linen to diffuse the daylight. He built a small, elevated platform, like a shrine the size of a double bed in the middle of the warehouse space, with stairs leading up to where he will lie. Standing, it reaches my waist.

"You okay amigo?" he asks.

I don't look at him but I half nod and pull a flexed smile to reassure him. I ignore the question but it fishhooks to my ribs.

Along the walls we place thick, tall candles. Our feet scuff the floor; our small noises echo off the ceiling and walls. The platform bed in the centre is a tiny raft in a vast white sea.

In the corner next to the washroom he has set up a white wooden chair and monitors for the three cameras he has mounted around the space. We hang another white tarp as a curtain, a corner where I will wait and watch, separate from what happens.

The first person will arrive at 6:00 pm. Then one every hour after that. They each get forty minutes. I will have just twenty minutes to reset, wipe the body clean, reposition it, check his pulse, and get a glass of water or use the toilet before the next person, already waiting in the hall outside. I cannot leave him alone with the people.

They will come in the door on the east side and leave through the door on the west side so others won't know. They have to sign this non-disclosure contract. And can't record the event in any way. I will wash the body in between to remove perfume or any smells so each person can begin with the scent of him. He has always smelled like clean laundry. Now I discover his natural odour comes from a cologne he bought in France. The bottle sits among the supplies. He suggests I dab a little on the smooth skin behind each of his ears after I wash him each time. A small bottle of familiarity. I note the name for later. In case I want to buy it.

He has placed a long wooden bench in the hall, like the kind in school hallways for kids to sit and tie their shoes, and had the painters paint it white, too. Those who wait can sit there until their turns.

He slumps to the floor to drink one of those liquid meals in a can. "No solids in my system," he explains. "So you're clear on how to do this?" he asks, looking around the room, scanning the details, not listening for an answer.

"Yes. I've been practicing." He takes another swig of the liquid protein drink. "On fruit."

"Don't worry," he says. "Even if you hurt me, it won't hurt for long." I find this no consolation.

"Are you sure?" I want to jump up and run away from my own question.

He pauses mid sip, scanning my face to see if I am asking about the pain or the whole endeavour. "Absolutely." An all-of-the-above lie. He clunks the drink down on the wood floor and leans sideways towards me, resting on a forearm. "Are you sure? Are you sure you can do this?" his eyes fixed on me, intent on an answer, and I simultaneously want to scramble towards and away from that blue.

"Absolutely." I have no certainty. The moments that will follow shadow puppet themselves in my mind, unimaginable. My hands curled hedgehog in my lap, what they will do, these hands pledged to care for him. It must be me.

Behind the curtain, I slough off my jeans and shirt, stand in my underwear, arms braced over my chest looking at the outfit he selected for me, a cotton outfit, medical-scrubs-type top and loose yoga pants. Something of ritual in the outfit, its white camouflage.

I slide them on and walk out from behind the curtain. He glances up at me, a laugh breaking out of his chest and bouncing around the room like thunder, shaking him.

Off my perplexed look, still laughing, tears now, he points at my crotch, then I realize my black underwear shows through. I'd blush but I am relieved, our laughter filling the cavernous space. A small thought that this can't happen now that laughter bounces around the space. And then his laughter subsides and he takes another sip of the can of liquid protein, shaking his head.

Behind the curtain again, I slide off the pants and my underwear, tugging on the pants, hoping the naked feeling will pass.

They are allowed to touch him. To even hit him if they need to. But nothing that will damage or alter his body. I police this. A baseball bat leans in the corner in case I need it. But he's asked me to hang back, appear invisible if I can. He wants each of these people to feel alone with him.

At 5:00 pm, the last preparations finished, even the futzing done, distractions abandon us. I stand, all in white, halfway between the platform and the door; he is perched in a white robe on the edge of the platform. We don't ask each other if we are certain anymore.

He takes a bottle of tequila and two glasses from his pack. Pours a silver finger's worth into both and hands me one.

"To the end . . . of beauty," he toasts. I mean to give him another flexed and determined smile, but it fractures, and I toss back the glass and turn it into a tequila grimace.

If I think about the fish in the aquarium at home, or about calling my mother, it seizes me, how surreal this is, what he asks of me. So I put these things from my mind.

At 5:30 pm we light candles around the warehouse. He removes his robe and the briefs, and then sits down on the table, placing a towel across his midriff. He hesitates, anxiousness betrayed in the jerkiness of his muscles as he lowers on to his back.

He closes his eyes. And I can look upon him. Some might attempt to measure his beauty, find it in the symmetry of his eyes, ears, the sharp cut of his jaw. Scientists once believed they could measure character in the dents and protrusions of the skull. I decide if I can find just one flaw I can get past his beauty. A birthmark, an age spot, a zit along his hairline. His beauty weighs upon me, unbearable and breathless in the vast space.

"Ready?" I ask, afraid of my own question. I pick up the tourniquet, see my hands shuddering, press them and the tourniquet into my lap to calm them.

He nods.

I tie the tourniquet around his left arm. I flex his arm then extend it looking for a vein. This is how the online tutorial video explained the procedure. My thumb presses into the palm of his hand, my hand bracketing his wrist.

"I"

can feel his pulse

"I just want to say"

flush as his eyes rise and incandesce, my heart a squirrel in the woodwork

"to say, whatever happens, I will protect you."

I release his hand, eyes retreat to the objects between us.

I pick up the needle and syringe in my right hand.

"I know."

I believe him.

The needle slips in easier than I thought, but the skin tugs with a resistance I never felt with the apple or the orange. I inject the liquid. I draw the needle out and quickly compress a cotton ball to the puncture wound with my thumb. I set the needle down, studying his closed eyes, mouth for any wince of pain. My left hand on his forehead, embracing his whole self with one hand, a thread as he disappears into the labyrinth alone.

The tension in his brow relaxes, his head tilts to the side. He's under. Down in the deep deep.

*Full fathom five . . . of his bones are coral made, nothing of him does fade, but doth suffer a change into something rich and strange.* A sonnet I memorized in grade twelve.

I lift my hand from his forehead. He lies before me, glowing in the candlelight. For a moment I am one of them, one of the people who will come here to see him, touch him anywhere, do anything. Less beautiful in stillness, perhaps, but more beautiful to behold uninterrupted. And vulnerable. I bring my mouth to his forehead, a long kiss to guard him against what comes next. Somewhere the air whispers in. The candles flicker.

AT 6:00 PM, the room crouches still and breathless. I lurch up, forcing air between my ribs, clad myself in the white surgical hat and mask. I will blend in with the white, become more invisible and less a witness. He also hopes that these will disguise me, take away the awkwardness if I know any of the people. I walk to the east door. I look back at him once, prone, Rodin-esque on the platform. It will all begin as soon as I open this door.

I grip the sliding door, yank it wide, squint to the blare of the harsh light bulbs in the long hallway. On the end of the long bench sits a woman, work suit, skirt, sunglasses. Her forehead furrows, confused by my mask and the white outfit perhaps. I hold out my hand palm up then gesture through the open door. She rises, her heels slow staccato on the wood floor, she walks into the shadows of the room and pauses just inside the door. Then she spots him, lying on the platform in the half-light.

"So this is really happening," she says and it's not really a question but I nod anyway.

"You can touch him anywhere and however you would like,"

I recite from rote the memo he emailed me. "Kissing, hitting, slapping are all permissible, but you must avoid any contact that might bruise." Her eyes are gripped to his unconscious body. "You must not block his airway. You must tell no one you were here or what happened. Once you sign this confidentiality agreement you will have forty minutes, no longer." She turns, seizes the clipboard, signs her name in a flourish, and thrusts it back without glancing at me. I retreat to the curtained corner where I watch her on the monitor, three alternating perspectives.

Poised before him, she extends one hand, like he might be a jack in the box, or a cruel trick. She then rests them both on his bare chest, her shoulders slumping with relief. She stands there for many moments. Then leans in, kisses him on the mouth. With an exhale, she simply rests her head on his chest, ear to rib cage, closes her eyes.

She lies there, draped across him, cheek hugging his chest. Five minutes drop off the clock. I expected more from her. After seven minutes I dig in my pack wondering where I put the book I brought for later after everyone is gone if I can't sleep. I can't focus on the words on the page, my eyes jumping up to the monitors every half a sentence in case I am missing something. I flip open the tiny notebook I brought to keep notes in, check my math on the drugs I injected, comb over the numbers.

Ten minutes. She only has thirty left. She's discarding time. I needlessly braced myself for jealousy. Though I do wish it was my cheek pressed against his chest right now.

Fifteen minutes. Her flesh turns to stone, melding with his, one work of art the curators will have to rename.

Thirty minutes. Why did I agree to this? What kind of sad man agrees to this agony and boredom?

Forty minutes, the digital clock on my phone nags. I rise from the chair, but before I can say anything, she arises, turns, as deliberately as she lay there with cheek to chest, a taste of a smile in her eyes but she disregards me, her heels punctuating a decisive rhythm barely broken when she shoves open the west door and leaves.

I balance and slosh the basin of warm water from the bathroom to the corner of the platform. I wipe him with a face cloth I keep warm and fresh from the basin. Just his face and chest. Through it all he sleeps the sleep of the vulnerable, a child's face, no residue in furrows or worry.

AT 7:00 PM, a man strides in the door, eyes fixed ahead on M's unconscious body, signs the contract without eye contact and then rushes to the platform, unbuttoning his shirt. He removes each article of his clothing, folding it before he attends to the next, a small pile of origami precision accumulates until he is standing naked facing M.

He climbs on top of the body, writhes on top with low growls as though he is trying to find a way in.

Only twenty minutes and he collapses on top of M. Heaving chest, gasping to regain his breath, he slides off M, unsteady on his feet, bracing himself against the platform. He shudders then, straightens up, and piece by piece he clads himself in the articles of clothing, snapping them out to unfold them before pulling them on, the pile diminishing. He leaves the air of the room, opens the door, with the same precision he folded his clothes. He still had ten minutes he could have used.

With a fresh basin of warm water and a cloth I wash the whole body this time, start with his hairline, precise, down his face and neck, behind his ears, rinsing the cloth every few wipes, gentle yet brusque enough to get clean, to erase any trace of the intensity.

**8:00 PM**. A woman. She signs the contract. I step back. She says no. No, she can't do this. It's too weird. Wrong. Sick. I remind her she's signed a confidentiality agreement. She nods. Looks at me with pity and horror, like this was all my idea. She bolts through the west door. I sit down in the corner, looking at the body on the monitor. I push my finger into the orange, peel it, then eat a segment. It's my practice orange, I recall mid chew. But I can't remember, was I the orange or was he?

**9:00 PM**. A woman who seems intent on running her hands over every spot on his body, even the unremarkable spots without names, the soft underbelly of his forearms, the smooth space behind his ears where his neck meets his skull. I empty the basin three times, washing him back to untouched.

**10:00 PM**. A man who only fondles and nuzzles the body's feet the whole time.

**AT 11:00 PM**, I grip the handle and throw my weight into sliding the door open. A man perched alone on the end of the bench waits in the glaring light of the long hallway. The last person of the night. His thin long limbs seem at odds with one another. I think I've seen him once before. He works with M. I gesture for him to go inside before he says anything.

My limbs lag heavy, my neck muscles slowly fusing my head rigid to my spine. I'm relieved he says nothing. I hold out the contract. Explain.

I close the door behind us as he signs, then I step back into the shadows, back into the corner. He throws a glance over his shoulder towards me, but sees I have abandoned him. He steps towards the table. Then he strides towards the table like he is about to jump into a cold lake.

He stops short. Beholds M's body in the waves of the candle-light.

I wonder if he will just stare at him for the whole forty minutes. He glances back towards me again, the white tarp curtain obscuring me. He hankers for only this, the illusion of privacy, then he leans in, holds his face in the crook of M's neck. I wonder if he is kissing M, wonder what he is feeling that close to the body. Does he feel the warmth of M's blood pulsing through his thick neck?

Then I realize what he is doing. Across the room I can hear him breathing, inhaling. He is smelling M. He broods his face from the neck to the armpit, gently inhaling. Then down the length of him to his midriff where he nuzzles in, almost grunting as he inhales. He continues to nuzzle the body; he is trying to rub the smells off on to himself.

I clear my throat when his forty minutes are up. Still fully clothed, he steps back and beholds M unconscious on the table once more.

"Thank you," he says, even though I am behind the drop sheet and he cannot see me. "I was afraid if I didn't get to go first he wouldn't smell like himself. You've done a beautiful job. He smells divine."

I smile firm in acknowledgment even though he can't see me. "You're welcome."

When he opens the east door to leave, he lets in a glimpse of the night, a distant streetlight, a car driving by, reminders of a real world we have given up.

I soak a clean cloth under the warm water of the tap at the small sink in the corner, fill the basin and steady it in my hands as I carry it to the body. I scrutinize the length of him, note his mussed hair, his limbs a fraction akimbo so he seems at odds, not restful. His chest fills and empties with undisturbed breaths. I straighten his legs, draw them closer together, roll his arms out so they lie palm up. I wipe the soft belly side of his limbs with care, the hairy sides more vigorously, in case the man has left scents of his own cologne, soap or body odour on him. With my fingers I comb M's hair back. I place my palm on his forehead again.

Behind the tarp, I find a stack of blankets in a bin of supplies he left there. I throw one over him, tucking it under, almost swaddling him. I slump to the floor next to the platform, facing him, sit with my hands around my bent knees in front of me, vigilant, the rise and fall of his breath guiding mine. Will he be tired? Or rejuvenated? His first appointment tomorrow isn't until 10:00 am, so he has time to sleep if he needs it.

I should sleep. The digital clock counts up, adrenalin fills my brain with pinball static. Will he ask what each of the people did? Will I tell him?

Around 1:30 am his fingers flicker, curl in a little, his head tilts a little to one side. I scurry softly to the back corner. I don't want to be right by his side when he wakes up. It could deliver the wrong message. I pick up the novel I brought, knowing I would never read it. I open it to page 132. I don't want him to know I've seen everything. I don't want him to worry.

"Hey," he says into the still, dark of the room.

"Hey," I say, standing. "Good morning. Sleep well?"

"Like a dead log. Not a single dream." The words echo in the room, mundane like misplaced bricks on the wood floor.

I hand him a glass of water. He holds the glass an inch from his mouth, as though he's remembering how to drink. I want him to drink, to wash the drugs out of his system. I need him to drink.

He drinks.

He tells me to sleep. I lie down on the cot in the shadows of the corner. I close my eyes, slowly slacken my breath and my jaw, fake deeper inhales despite the thudding of my pulse in my throat and ears. His bare feet slap across the wood floor to the bathroom. The slush of water, then hissing, sloshing sound of him soaping and rinsing himself. Raspy sounds of towel on skin, he pads out of the bathroom with the towel tucked around his waist, ponders the novel I left on the chair, carries it to the platform and flops down with it, fingering the pages to the beginning in the dim light. I avidly watch him read, waiting for the brush of his fingers turning the pages, and sleep slips in between those turns.

IN THE MID-MORNING LIGHT, the room glows. The muted whites of the bedding, the glaring whites of the walls, all refracting light, I wake to a room in heaven, or some 1970s movie version of heaven. Then I remember.

I smell coffee, then notice him holding up a cup to me.

"Coffee to wake you up before I put you to sleep?"

He shakes his head smiling, adds, "Shithead."

9:30 am, he paces near the platform as though on the edge of a pool, shrugs off the robe and folds it, shucks off his boxers, folds them and puts them on top of the robe, sliding onto the platform and drawing the hand towel over his midriff in one quick, almost modest move. He shuffles his limbs, settling on the platform, then cocks his head towards me, winking a half smile.

I tie the tourniquet around his arm, pat the flesh, looking for a vein. Find it. Inject the drugs. Remove the needle, holding my fingers over the spot.

"Do I get a lollipop, doctor?" he asks.

I give him a doctor's humourless smile.

In my periphery, I see his eyebrows peak a little, his eyes

narrowing and scrutinizing my face. I think he's going to ask me if I am okay. But he doesn't. That's too dangerous a question now.

I cup a hand on his forehead, tether us. Wait until I feel the slackening, his head lull, his muscles giving way. Alone.

I look up at the clock. How did I pass a whole half hour sitting here with him? It's time.

**10:00 AM.** A woman, maybe forty-five. She's dressed for work, hair pinned back into a tight ponytail, the colour of horse chestnuts on asphalt, a white-collared blouse and pencil skirt. She undoes a button on the waist of her skirt, then slides the zipper down and steps out of it, holding it with one hand then draping it over the corner of the platform. Unbuttons her blouse, then drapes it, too. She is standing before him in only her bra, panties, and heels. She steps out of her heels and climbs the steps up the foot of the platform, sinks down on all fours, crawling up until she is even with him. Then, she with the grace of ritual, lowers a shoulder, turns over and rests upon him, her back to his chest.

"He's so warm," she says. She reaches down and grabs his slack hands, pulls them around her midriff, her head sinking back into the crook between his head and shoulder. She strains her chin towards the ceiling, then nestles her head on the other side of his thick neck. She torques her head back and away to see his face, gazes at him.

She flips over, nuzzling her cheek into his neck, her legs falling to his flanks, straddling him. She pushes up, restless, discontent with any of these positions. She is astride his midriff, shoulders hunched, she stares him down, eyes pinched, unslaked.

Flips back to her back, head thrown back to the crook of his neck. Then slides off and stands leaning against the platform, legs tense.

She leans her face in closer to his and with the thumbs of a thief she slides open his eyes.

I can't see her face in the monitor, and her back shields her from my corner of the room.

Then, a thumb to each eyelid, she shutters them closed, kisses first one then the other.

She steps back, pauses barefoot in her bra and panties as I study her stance, at a loss to what she desires. Skirt, blouse, heels slide into place. She removes a mirror from her handbag and checks her face. Maybe to see if any of this has stained her. Maybe to make sure she's still the woman she was when she walked in here.

She turns to me in the corner. Though she can't see me through the hanging tarp, it feels like she looks directly at me. "Thank you."

**11:00 AM.** A young man, muscular. He might be M's workout partner. Must have a penchant for muscles, because he keeps squeezing M's. Then he gives up, sits back on his haunches, maybe disconcerted that the unconscious cannot flex. He draws M's opposite arm across his body, pulls him onto his side, extends his arms above his head, and manages to pull M over onto his stomach. He seems disturbingly proficient with unconscious bodies; I hope he's a nurse. He climbs astride M's buttocks, runs his hands over and over M's lat muscles, his back muscles, then mashes his face into the flesh of M's back, nuzzling, jerking himself fiercely over the small of M's back. Spasms like seizure. He stares down at the mess he's made, a grim sadness pulling down the sides of his mouth. Hurriedly sluffs himself and M off with a damp towel from his gym bag, then rushes out the door.

**12:00 – 6:00 PM**. I lose track of the order. People become un-remarkable. A handful of men jack off, running their thick paws up and over the body, nuzzling maws into his crotch, his armpits. A handful of women lie on top of the body. Some touch themselves, some do not. One cries. I imagine she's left salt on his skin.

**6:00 – 7:00 PM**. I order ginger chicken and green beans in black bean sauce. I meet the deliveryman at the downstairs door, the sky, disturbingly real behind him. He takes too long futzing in his pockets for change, M left unattended, so I wave for him to keep the change and I spring back up the stairs, sliding the door open, closed behind me and locking it. In the bathroom with the fan whirring I devour the food, voracious. I don't want the smell of the Chinese takeout to persist in the room where M lies unconscious.

The containers empty, my hunger persists. But I wrap the packages back up in the plastic bag, tie the handles tightly, lean out the back door and drop the bag on top of the bins guarding the wall below.

Back inside, I scrub my hands under the taps, my lips, water from the tap as hot as I can tolerate. I inject him again to ensure he does not become conscious before the end of the night. I check his heart rate and blood pressure. Both acceptable. I scrutinize his face, looking to see if he has been in any way affected by what has happened over the duration of the day. A Mona Lisa mouth stares back at me. I want to see sadness. But I see nothing substantial. Maybe he would enjoy this. Now more than ever, I can't pretend to know what he wants.

**7:00 – 11:00 PM.** A few become distinct. The one who has to have his fingers in the body's mouth. The one who has to sit on the body's face. With both I zoom in on the monitors to ensure they will not suffocate him, that his chest still rises and falls unimpeded.

One brings her own toy. She uses it to pretend the body is penetrating her. A few bring cameras, but I confiscate the memory cards and videotapes if they manage to get a shot or two.

Between each, I pour a fresh basin of warm water, balance its sloshes to the platform with the soap he normally uses, and a cloth to clean him, always returning him to the same position, on his back, facing the ceiling. I wash him even if there is no visible mess. I wash him so I know he is clean again.

11:00 pm. I close the door behind the last man, the one with the hairy back and the intense need to lick M's ears.

I lock the door, a few steps towards the platform and I slump to the floor, sitting, fall forward on my legs, hugging my knees. Shudder. The room feels chilled. And M is exposed, naked to the air. I lean to the side and push up to standing, gangly, stagger to get the soap and water.

A fresh basin of water, I wipe him down, but his skin is warm, my hands cold. I scrub him with the washcloth thoroughly. Things I have learned from washing him: he has a scar, half an inch, almost invisible beside his left knee cap; underneath his chin is a spot the size of a dime where no beard stubble grows; under the skin of his left palm haunts a speck, perhaps graphite from a pencil in elementary school or a dot of gravel from a childhood fall. I know his body more now. But I see I know him less.

With a clean towel I dry him off. I throw a blanket over him again. I have a long shower. The water against the nape of my neck shuts off my thoughts. I am unconscious under the rushing water. I might never get out.

"Hey!" I hear him call. "Don't use all the hot water!" I know he's partly joking. But I want him to have a good long shower too. So I finish up.

**HE DRINKS A LIQUID MEAL** while I eat another orange, resigning myself to cannibalism via fruit. I ask him if he's tired. He takes a moment to respond. "Weary." And I think, yes, this is a much better word. I will wear it too.

I say goodnight, though I don't want to leave him now that he's here. I fall shoulder first into the corner cot. And this time I do sleep. A dreamless sleep crushes me in the sagging cot, almost violent in its dreamlessness. Like the dreams might have been there but were torn away as I woke up, gulped whole.

**7:23 AM.** I wake up to the thick hiss of the shower, slip under into sleep again, then wake to the sound of his bare, wet feet slapping across the floor. Groggy, I ask if he slept. He shakes his head. We have just over half an hour until the first person arrives. He tosses his towel on the platform, slides on some clean underwear and then towels his hair more, mutters he's ready when I am. I can put him under any time. And this is how Sunday will go. Each of us a little impatient for this to be over. For the weary part to end.

**10:00 AM TO 1:00 PM.** Another foot fetishist. Then a woman who cries much of the time, touching his cheeks with her shaky hands, like she half expects him to cry too. A guy who lies between M's legs, his face mashed into M's chest as he finishes himself off. All pretty usual.

**1:00 PM**. A different story. The man arrives like an awful sugges-tion. He smacks M's placid face. My body goes rigid. A smack is not enough for me to stop the man. I grip the edges of my chair. I eye the bat leaning against the wall in the corner, picture myself smashing this man in the jaw with it, watching him fall to the floor. I can barely stop myself from wanting to hurt this man back. Even though M specifically warned me this might happen. Someone might want to hurt him. And he specifically stipulated that hurt was permissible unless it became harm. Smacking does little more than redden the face.

He smacks him again. The other side of the face.

And then he kisses him. A hard kiss. Almost grinding. I try to breathe in. The man climbs on top of the body. Then with one hand he pounds on the body's considerable chest as he jacks him-self off in a peculiar jerking, yanking motion. He is bordering on harm. I want to hurt him. I sit in the corner, my hands clenched.

When he slams out the back door, I rush to M. I wash the body, searching in the dim light. There might be bruises later.

I rest my ear on his chest. Listen to the heartbeat. He told me to check his heart rate through the day. I can almost pretend this is all I am doing. I am resting my head against his chest. This could happen while watching a movie, resting in bed before sleep, after sleep, at the beach. But we don't have a movie, bed, or beach, so I do it here, like this.

**THE NEXT WOMAN** is like an angel lying down with stray dogs and hungry ghosts. She signs the contract. The room becomes about her. All the dust motes turn their faces towards her. She stands halfway between the door and him, her purse held in front of her. I don't know whether to say anything else, to encour-age her. I decide to just sit in the corner and let her be. Though I can't help but lean around the hanging tarp and watch her as she stands tall, like Alice growing from drinking the wrong bottle.

"I know what you're thinking," she says like she's talking to him, not me. "You think I am one of the ones who disapproved of this. But you're wrong." She wanders to the platform, shifts to sit on the edge next to him, sways her legs. "I was one of the first to reply. The chance to look at him. Really look at him. I've known him a long time and in all that time I've only ever glimpsed him. I told a friend of mine, I know I know. I know we're not supposed to tell. But I had to tell one person. She was horrified. She said this was pure objectification."

She slides off the table and rounds to the other side of him, a waltz in knife sharpening. Her grace is disconcerting.

She gazes over him, leans forward, angling to mirror his horizontal face, mouth inches from his mouth.

"That was the word she used: 'butchery.' Like dissecting a frog in science class."

I lean into the monitors, waiting for her to kiss him.

"Like this is any less him. Like to scrutinize is to lose his essence. I look at this space behind his ear and I see all of him. I run my hand along here, here where the front muscle meets the back muscle, like currents in a river, and I think this is more him than anything he could ever say. I see everything in this place. The first time he ran in his backyard, ran instead of walked, to the way he might strain with his legs, weaving them with some-one else's. This spot here. This spot is everything. And so is this one. He is thick with himself. If he were to wake up right now, we could talk about the weather, he could speak any number of nonsense words. The body, his body tells me so much more."

She turns to look at me. She's not shy. She wears the clothes of a shy woman, but she is not shy.

"I want some time with him now. Alone."

"I can't."

"For me. I promise I won't hurt him. You know me now. You know I won't hurt him."

"I can't. What do you want to do?"

"Nothing. Maybe. Or something."

"I don't understand."

"Yeah, no, that's not it. See, I am not sure I have ever really looked at him. I mean I've glanced and maybe even made eye contact, but . . . we don't. We don't look at people. The more we love them, the less we look. As though looking would make them love us less or take away that love. Because then they'd know, wouldn't they. Then they'd see the unbearable longing." She looks down at her feet and then back up at him. "I just . . . I just want to look. Purely look. Without him seeing me. Without you seeing me."

"You'll hardly notice me. It's like I'm invisible."

"Maybe. Maybe it would have been like that if we'd never spoken. But now I know you. You're the one in the corner with all your own particular reasons for being here. And I'll be thinking about them. Instead of mine. I promise. I promise I will treat him preciously. I won't leave a trace."

On three monitors, from three different angles, she grabs hold of his hand with both of hers, she beholds him, with such a reverence, such raw tenderness. Sure, I think the only reason she talked to me was so I'd break this rule, that I would talk to her and destroy the anonymity. Regardless, she's right. It can't be the same.

"Okay," I say. "But only ten minutes. And you can't tell anyone. Particularly him."

I am betraying him. But I guess I already did when I spoke to her. This could just remedy the problem.

I step outside the west side door so that anyone waiting at the east side entrance won't see me, won't know I've broken the rules for someone. The door closes. I don't have a key for the back door. The door automatically locks behind me and I don't have a key. I lose my breath for a moment. I am in her hands, for better or for worse. And so is he.

I watch my watch closely. When ten minutes arrive, they predictably, and horribly pass to eleven. I start searching the wall above me, looking for a window low enough, or another door I might not have seen before.

Twelve.

Thirteen.

Fourteen. I'm sure she's killed him.

Fifteen. I need to break in, destroy any evidence that I've been here.

Sixteen. An odd thing he wanted, to be sure, but doable. Until I destroyed it. I wonder if I unconsciously wanted to destroy it.

Seventeen. She opens the door, her face soft, a little sad.

"That's done."

I can't berate her. I see on her face. She's experienced my entire weekend in seventeen minutes. Now she knows. I want her to tell me M chose the right person. Tell me I was right to do this.

But she just hugs me in a light forlorn embrace and she clunks down the stairs. I want to watch her go, but I need to make sure he's okay and rush back in.

I scrub him thoroughly, harder than I have, check backs of legs and arms for bruises or any signs of harm. Nothing.

**ALMOST THE LAST ONE**. We look like we could be related, same hair colour, roundness of features, a plain but cute face. Same awkward combination of self-consciousness and assumed invisibility — a neurotic paradox. He blushes as he signs the contract, his face raw, transparent and hungry. He's more me than me. His skinlessness is unbearable. I know now why I drive some people to anxious distraction, waltzing through the world all soft underbelly. He takes cautious steps closer to M's body. Like a child walks into traffic. I retreat to the corner. I try not to watch him. I watch him. He thrums with all he wants.

His hand rests sudden and awkward on the body's chest. An awkward first date, he takes small gulping steps into oblivion, his childhood fantasies for the school's hot jock, all his unrequited loves like knives falling from a drawer far above. And then his cheek pressed to that broad chest. His face contorted. Pain. Awe.

I can't look.

I can't stop looking.

An awful thing, this. Seeing myself, making a fool of myself. For me to see. Yet he doesn't hold back. Maybe we're not alike after all. Maybe we have nothing in common. I try not to watch. I give him no more than a few glances, a montage of diminishing returns: the crown of his head burrowing against M's clavicles; he's on top of the body, seated as if on a motorcycle; then he lies on top, struggling to put its arms around him.

Then I can't tell what he's trying to do. He has the body on its side. He wrestles with the body, pulling a limb over himself, rocking back and forth as though to get momentum, but the body rolls back onto its back. I shouldn't, but I decide to help. He seems oblivious to me standing beside the table. He doesn't look at me. And then I see what he's trying to do. He's trying to get under the body. He wants it to lie across the length of him. I understand this, his desire to be held down. I have a small catalogue of moments like this in my history. A mechanic with a v-shaped back; the lawyer with the desire to pin with his long limbs; the actor who could only be held down, never return the favour.

I see what this man is trying to do. And I want to do it too. So I step forward and take hold of M's arm. I say nothing. I don't want to interrupt the dream. I just want to help. Together we turn the body. He lies face down beside it and we pull it up on top of him. I pause, making sure the body won't roll off. The table is wide enough that the body won't roll off onto the floor so that's fine. I step back slowly. I hear laughter. Small chuckling laughter. The body shakes a little on top of the man. Not laughter. Weeping. Breathless, suffocating weeping. I don't ask him if he's okay. I sit behind the curtain, chin to my chest, and listen to his sobs.

**THE COUPLE**. She tells me that each of them will take twenty minutes. She touches a button on her watch and faces the door they came in, stands a foot from it while he takes his turn, not swaying from it even once. At twenty minutes an alarm on her watch protests the silence and she glances at it to verify. She strides over to where I sit behind the tarp and asks me for a wet cloth. Over her shoulder I see her husband pulling his pants back on. She washes the body quickly, gently, while her husband takes his position two feet from the exit door, tucking in the last of his shirt, then standing, staring unflinching at the door. Her first moan, his eyes stray from the door slightly, and then when he hears the slap of skin on skin behind him. But still, he does not turn around. When she's finished, dressed, she strides to his side, he nods, then opens the door for them, letting her exit first. I can't help but wonder how the rest of their day goes.

**I POUR WATER** into the basin one last time, wipe him down. Then I fall back onto the chair behind the tarp, eyes closing weary.

Last light diminishes behind the cotton window coverings, noise of traffic in the distance fades. The numbers on the digital clock count up, glacial.

I hear him clear his throat, see on the monitors as his limbs reach, stretch out, groggy from the medication. I can feel what he feels, the alcohol splash burn of consciousness, the room bleached of colour, the pain of moving even a little.

I distract myself by drawing a glass of water from the tap for him. I hear a noise. I open the door to the hallway and see four people waiting there. The man who smacks, the woman who left without doing anything, and two miscellaneous others. They have come back, slouched and tense. They look at me expectantly. I shake my head. They look down or away, collect their raincoats, satchels, briefcases. I go back in, close the door.

"How many?" he asks, slumped. The light in the room has changed, softened.

"They're leaving."

I sit down beside him. Waiting for one of us to admit defeat.

"Fewer than before," he says, then sighs, and he lies back on the plank floor. His skin looks less pale, pink of blood flow returning to his neck and cheeks. I can hardly see the scratch where the woman slipped and dragged her fingernails down his ribs. His breathing is deeper, his chest rising. I want to lay my head upon his chest.

"What will you do now?"

"I'm leaving." His head lolls towards me.

"What? Where are you going?"

"I've found a place. I think I'll seem wrongly shaped to them. People will still notice me probably, but it'll be different. I'll appear freakish."

"You can't just step out of your life like that, and what if you're wrong. I mean, you were wrong about this."

I think I've wounded him, but his eyes study my face, like he's trying to gauge carefully his next words. "You see, right?"

I don't know what he's referring to. Shadows pool in the corners, the room needing some candlelight.

"You know why I asked you."

My stomach falls.

I can't look at him. His voice is all around me. I am those famished dogs in the hallway waiting. I am worse. Because I need him that way. Famished dogs aren't supposed to dream of love.

"It's . . . it's nothing."

"Put me under once more."

"No, no that's just stupid." I get up and pad to the corner behind the curtain, shuck off the whites and yank on my street clothes.

"It's your turn."

"I don't need a turn." I throw the white clothes into a pack. "I've humoured you on this, but I really think you might have lost it."

"Then I will inject myself." He picks up the needle and the syringe. "You won't leave me. You will stay to watch over me. And then it's your choice. But you know I am lying here for you."

"You're insane."

He reaches for the needle and syringe. He looks down at his arm. He can't bring himself to do it. This might be his last anguish. I don't need to touch him. But I can just let him think I did. I rush to where he sits, hold out my hand for the syringe.

"Let me."

In my periphery, he scrutinizes my countenance, but I don't take my eyes off the syringe.

He lies back.

The needle goes in easily. I have become proficient.

His body prone, head tilted back, throat bare. The hallway people gone. The seconds, the breaths, the thin orange air, the white wash floor all thrum. I can desecrate and be done with this desire. Or I can let this longing live on, whatever agony it will become. His head slumps to the side, limbs exhaling.

I don't know how they all did it. How did they know what to do? I am a lesser person. I do not know what I want.

I need time to think. I turn him on his side. It takes all my strength this time, afraid of what comes next. I lie down face to face with him. We are brackets facing one another on the narrow table. I need time to think how I can be done with this. He is just sleeping. His mouth, his soft breath, the moment ceaseless. We are lovers, you see. He is leaving in the morning. For good. But for now he is just sleeping, next to me, in my bed. No end. He is leaving in the morning. We are lovers, you see. There is no end. I need more time.

# THREAD FOR
# SLEEPWALKERS

# THREAD FOR SLEEPWALKERS

**THE ATTENDANT TELLS HER** to lie back, relax. Her neck stiffens. Who lies down like this, she wonders. This is how robots lie back to sleep. What colour is the ceiling trying to be? What would she call it? Bland mint. Surgical calm. Algae water. Tasteless, but she can see a spot where the painters didn't apply enough paint so the primer shows through. This was someone's take on a dream world. Their watery, minty, flawed dreams.

She has two hours and they'd like to see if she naps, observe what her brainwaves do. She can tell them what these brainwaves do. They stagger, they struggle, they collapse, but they do not sleep. She's exhausted. The day tastes like a mouthful of pennies. But she doesn't feel like sleeping. Worse, her brain latches to him in the hallway, a year since their last collision. Now she will see him every two hours as she exits the sleep study room and he re-enters, then vice versa: they pass each other headed the other way, as though on opposite escalators gripped in their own ups or downs.

He looked good. Hair shorter, more grey, haunted below the eyes a little, but thinner. He's lost some weight. He was carrying a children's magazine and she was carrying a book, some random book her sister-in-law gave her because she found it hilarious. But she doesn't find it funny, the book like one of those people who try too hard because they have this idea of themselves as funny. She hates having to humour a novel.

He looked like his arms would fall off from the awkward feelings of seeing her, so she leaned in and put one arm around him, a half-hearted hug. Better than a no-hearted one she thinks. She smiled at him as part of her brain, the part at the back it felt like, struggled to remember why they broke up. Dredged up the short hand version and even dipped into the long hand version while she asked how he'd been. Part of her, her sternum part, leaned a little forward towards the gap in his shirt, the little flash of chest hair there making her think of his chest, beastly and warm, naked in their bed, her arm resting tame on it, rising and falling.

She startles awake, looks at her watch. She slept for an hour and a half. The attendant knocks as he opens the door. She doesn't remember him leaving. He gently unplugs the electronic leads from her one by one, small jerking motions. She wants to apologize to him for wasting his time. She wonders for a moment if she made it all up, the insomnia.

The attendant leads the way to the door, and, as soon as he turns back to the room, she hurriedly combs her hair with her fingers and stretches her face and scrunches it up hoping to get some colour back into it.

He's waiting in the hallway, waiting for his turn. Or maybe for her.

"Hi," she says, scanning his expression, not sure whether she should continue walking or whether they might talk.

"Sleep well?" he asks, joking.

"Yes," she replies, a little crestfallen to admit she's failing so badly at insomnia. "You?" she shakes her head, "I mean, of course you didn't sleep. You were waiting. I mean how was —" she gestures towards the waiting area, a blush of foolishness smattering her neck and cheeks.

"Good good," he gives a small life-preserver smile.

The sleep clinic attendant calls him from the lab. He must go and sleep now. And she must go to the waiting area they call a lounge and humour the book a little and spend more time rehashing the past catalogue of complaints and grievances, her interrogations, his retreats. And she's sure, so sure, that he's not rehashing, probably not even remembering. Probably even now, already, sleeping. And she wonders, what does a man who has no problem sleeping want with a sleep clinic? Maybe they're studying him to find out his secrets, or to rob him of some of his sleep to give to others. Maybe he's providing a sleep donation. She could be his sleep beneficiary. Would she accept his donation? Would it come with his peculiar dog dreams? Hell, she'd take Mussolini's sleep if she could get it.

There are no couches in the "lounge," just hard wooden chairs. But lounging, she guesses, is a slippery slope to dozing, then, even worse, sleeping. The sleep clinic people probably don't want sleep to happen if it's not on their watch. They want to contain and study it. Scrutiny and evaluation aren't great sleep aids, though. Usually.

He's in there sleeping, she frets, and he's not thinking of me. And then it occurs to her that in two hours she will see him again, as they pass one another on the threshold between sleep and consciousness. So she opens her book and begins to read, her mouth set grimly against the book's desire to be funny. She will give herself enough time to go to the washroom before then. Maybe a little blush. Aim for effortless effort. No one dresses up and wears makeup for a sleep clinic. That would be like getting fancy for bedtime. And she doesn't want her interest to be obvious. Damn, her interest.

She puts her attention to the book. In that back part of her brain where she is sorting through the forgotten reasons they broke up, a nonsense part of her decides that the sleeplessness caused it and how, every time she'd turn over during the night, he'd be sleeping too well. He could sleep anywhere. In planes, moving vehicles in general (the vibrations he said), in cafés, in movies, at dinner tables. When they first started dating, his narcolepsy embarrassed her. Until her friends could see he just slept a lot and that it wasn't a judgment on the quality of their company. Still, his lowered head, the soft snoring, always disappointed her so.

The clock in the hall tells her it's almost time. She washes her hands in the bathroom, sorts her hair, combs her fingers through again, and runs a finger with lip balm on her lips. She decides it all looks good without looking like effort. She takes a deep breath, pulls open the bathroom door and ambles down the hallway, pausing to look at the bulletin board, staggering her pace, not wanting to be waiting outside the door when he exits.

These are wide hallways. So much space. Imagine if you could save that space and give it to someone in need. A child in Bangalore. She doesn't know if children in Bangalore need more space. She's not even quite sure where Bangalore is. Still, the hallway is wide enough she could lie down and raise her arms above her head, point her toes and still not touch either wall, caught Tantalus in between.

She warns herself to keep it short, say only a handful of things then say "I should be getting in there," or "Sleepy time." No, that's too cute. She needs to leave him wanting more.

She had always failed to negotiate longing with him. With other men she could rile them up, distract them, sometimes just a matter of standing in their personal space, then departing for another room. Irregularly and erratically offering them what they want. With him she couldn't begin to know what he desired. He seemed to have his head in a sack most of the time. Then he'd all of a sudden lean in, the bristles on his jaw tickling her neck. She had no way of knowing when he'd lean into her again, no way to encourage him to want that. Maddening. So why was she even trying now?

Twenty feet from the door, she decides she'll pace the hallway until he comes out. He'll be that guy the sleep clinic technician has to wake at the end of every session. The only guy. She could have volunteered. She had a bit of a history of waking him up. They'd only been together for a year, but she spent much of that time waking him. Sometimes he'd even deny he'd been sleeping. Drool in the corner of his mouth, his eyes barely open, "I wasn't. I just closed my eyes."

Just closed his eyes. Towards the end she felt she knew how people who had loved ones in comas felt. Love for the absent yet present. And a vague suspicion he was doing this on purpose. Like if she could be more interesting, more stimulating he wouldn't always be slipping down into slumber. Well, she doubted the loved ones of coma victims felt specifically that way, but she could relate at least to the part about loving someone absent.

The door. The shadow of a beard, a half drunk, sleep staggered look as he swerves to walk down the hall towards her. She stops her pacing, smiles at him when he sees her.

"Sweet dreams," he says and she feels the hitch of disappointment, that he has begun and ended their conversation before she could do either. She gives him a weaker smile and goes into the lab, into its muted, watery light.


**HE GOES TO THE MACHINE**, the coffee and tea one. The bastard thing only sells decaf. Predictable and irritating. He hasn't slept in twenty-four hours. Damn clinic. The motor vehicle branch insisted he come. When he was here last time the doctor thought he had seen something, something that might be a sign of narcolepsy, so now the motor vehicle branch was demanding a follow up. He doesn't have time for this. He knows if they find anything in this round of tests they'll make him keep coming back, suspects they might even take his license. He needs his license.

He has a scheme. The last time they'd noticed something, so this time he's determined he won't fall asleep. No caffeine, no chocolate, no soda of any kind, they said. All of those were pretty visible contraband anyways. Not the chocolate-covered coffee beans he's slipped into the pocket of his chinos. He might have built up a tolerance to them though, feels groggy even now.

In the couple of hours between sleep sessions they leave you to wander the hallways and hang in the lounge. Plenty of time to chow down on some of those beans. He is careful not to eat so many he'll shake or seem jittery. Just enough so he won't fall asleep. Even then he has to take to rolling onto his stomach. They don't know he can't sleep on his stomach. He just has to stay awake. He needs his driver's license.

So strange to see her here. Guess it's been about ten months or something. Last Halloween maybe. Yeah. She looks good. A little tired. Not surprising, he chuckles. She always seemed a bit wound up. He can't remember ever seeing her sleep. She'd come to bed after him and wake up before him. For all he knew, she never slept. He remembers a movie, one of those fancy dress films, where the guy watched the woman peacefully unconscious in the bed next to him. That would have been nice. Hell, even to see her just relax for five minutes, stop being so jittery and watchful.

She was always watching him. Like they were taking dance lessons and she was waiting for his next step. Made it pretty difficult to take a next step.

Two coffee beans from his pocket. No one watching. He forgot to check for surveillance cameras in the hallways or lounge. Nothing visible. Maybe they've installed hidden ones, but they wouldn't really have much use for them; most people don't come here to avoid sleeping. But he knows he's not narcoleptic.

He's never fallen asleep at the wheel. One time with the work truck, yeah, but he was really sick. And he blacked out, didn't fall asleep. He doesn't have a problem. He just has to stay awake.

He can feel the sleep rumbling in, like walls of water have flooded the hall, the rooms, his limbs too heavy to move through the weight of the drowsiness and the slow, increasing undertow, so he sinks to a wooden chair, looks at the floor with longing, the peaceful ocean floor where the currents would cease and he could float, nudging the sandy bottom.

He slips two more coffee beans in his mouth. Damn hard staying awake this last time. He'd had to dig his fingernails into his palm, bite the inside of his cheek. He couldn't get caught trying to hold his eyes open. He just has to make it through the day.

Maybe her hair is a little different. Something is a little different but he can't put his finger on it. She looks good. But he remembers that gnawing way she always seemed a little disappointed, that graven mouth like she'd hoped for a little more. He remembered, standing there at the Halloween party her friend Mindy threw, looking at her dressed as a schoolteacher and looking down at the costume she'd chosen for him. She'd dressed him as a schoolboy, a troublesome schoolboy complete with shorts, suspenders, and a dunce cap. It all felt so . . . literal. When they got home she cried, said she was sorry she put so much effort into the costumes. How she thought he had a fantasy about librarians. But she didn't know there was a difference between a schoolteacher and a librarian. A big difference.

He went to bed while she was still uncoiling and unpinning her Halloween schoolteacher bun. That night he couldn't fall asleep. Tossed and turned. She didn't come to bed. And he thought to himself that if his one chief pleasure in the world was sleep and this woman was making him sleepless, then things weren't right at all. So in the morning, at the breakfast table, he explained how he was going to sleep at his friend Dave's place and how he was then going to get his own apartment. Even as he was saying this, one part of his brain was thinking about what kind of bed he would get in his new place. He knew he should be paying attention — tears dripping into her cereal, the washed blue pleading of her eyes intent on him — but that other part of his brain was thinking he might get a single bed. Something about a single bed seemed serious about sleep. Monastic.

She hadn't said anything. Looked at her cereal bowl, the cereal half eaten and taking on milk. When he finished telling her what he had to say she'd gotten up, plunked her dish in the sink and retreated to the bedroom. Not a word.

He doesn't remember her saying another word after that. Until now, in the sleep clinic hallways. Cracked smile, he almost forgets to try to stay awake he feels so good. Like fleece good. She's one of those people, he guesses now, who you don't know you're missing until you see them. How a mouthful of water can show you you've been thirsty. Maybe she's getting help for being wired all the time. They could sleep together then. Rolled up in sleep and blankets, the hibernation they never had. Just a day when they didn't leave bed. She never understood that dream. He has to pee. And he should comb his hair. Make himself not just a collection of leached pale skin and mussed hair.

The glimpse. Like she wanted to say more. In that instant, all the persistent, famished questions she ever asked him cloyed like wet sneakers. He had wanted to talk to her too. He'd been thinking about her lying there in the sleep lab. Thinking he should say something to her. But then he saw her, that anxious glance, hope, her cheeks rosy with it. And all he could say was "sweet dreams," and escape down the hallway.

Now, an hour away from that moment, he wishes he could put the dunce cap back on and sit in the corner. Well, he wishes he could make her a little less available so he would respond differently.

In the bathroom, he grimaces at the sallow face hanging in the mirror. Bad lighting probably but he looks grey as aged beef. Grey with a little green. Turns out sleep labs might not be the best place to impress a girl, strung out on chocolate-covered espresso beans, ragged with fatigue. He runs the tap, splashes some water on his face, then combs a wet hand through his hair, thinner than when he saw her last. She wouldn't notice things like that. She's a better person than he is. Some people must find that tolerable. Dating a better person than yourself. He has a hard time stomaching it. Always feeling somehow wrong, or like he is doing things not quite right. At a certain point he became allergic to trying. "Sweet dreams." The mouse sitting in the maze, not trying.

This is how he feels in the sleep lab. Like a mouse in a large maze, the piece of cheese off in some other room. Like maybe they even brought her in here to test him. What kind of test would that be? A test after the fact, long after, to see if he remembers why he chose sleep over her. Left turn or right at the next corner. Or sit right where you are, refuse the test. That seems to make the most sense to him now.

On the table in the lounge, a *Good Housekeeping*. And a kid's magazine with a maze on the back. Everything is a maze he thinks. Most of the children's games are about getting out. But he remembers the myth about the Minotaur was about getting in and then back out. He doesn't remember why the guy went into the maze. The labyrinth. But who would go willingly. Maybe it was a challenge, but mostly if you enter a place you know is designed to get you lost, you deserve what you have coming to you.

Two, maybe three more of these lab sessions and he can get out of here. He holds onto the kid's magazine with the maze.

A reminder. Don't go into the maze. He picks up the *Good House-keeping* and reads an article on organizing a kitchen drawer using Ziplocs. Makes sense. Practical. Things feel better in a Ziploc. Most things. When he traveled to Mexico that time he put everything in Ziplocs. His underwear, his socks, his toothbrush. Everything contained from everything else. He remembers how vindicated he felt when he opened the pack in the hotel room and discovered how the shaving cream decided to leak during the trip and filled its Ziploc but left all the other pack items clean and clear. It had been the right thing to do. That was the trip just after Halloween, after he broke up with her. He went in November by himself. An awkward and desperate trip. He couldn't look at the travel photos of him, pasty white, a smile clutching his face.

He looks at the grimacing clock on the wall. Time to go back in. Should he say something this time. Something more than "sweet dreams." He ponders as he walks down the hallway towards the sleep lab. And then the door opens, she steps out, hair a little tousled, a flinch of a smile. "Sweet dreams," she says, passes him, padding on down the hallway, not looking back.

**SHE'D SLEPT AGAIN**. Maddening. After all these sleepless nights, to finally get into the sleep lab to show them her insomnia, and what does she do? She sleeps. She can't explain it. The low light of the room, the non-dreamy paint scheme, the murky blue glow off the monitors, all soothed her. Even the technician, Saul, soothed her. He was a nice man, too young for her to be sure, but sweet, attentive. And she liked the way he re-attached the leads, checked the monitor and watched over her, a kind squinty-eyed smile when she turned his way. A little concern, a little interest. He was good at his job. She didn't get the feeling that she was the 345th person he had monitored. Yes, she felt like he had seen people sleep, but he would make sure she slept safely. She must have fallen asleep before he left the room again. He was an insomnia cure. Him and his watchfulness. Damn him.

She struggles to blink awake, grumpy her sleep's been interrupted again, just when she finally had some. She pushes out the sleep lab door, pondering sleeping on the lounge floor. Then him again. "Sweet dreams," is all she can think to say.

Surprises herself. She feels angry with him, an old anger with an easy groove she slips easily into. She carries it down the hallway with her to the bathroom. She has to pee. She has to wash her face. And she wants to carry this a little further. It surprises her. She didn't realize she was angry with him. Well, she'd been pissed when he broke up with her, but in the weeks that followed the weather had changed on that, with moments of feeling freer and gasps of relief. An unaffectionate narcoleptic man is not something you dwell on losing, she'd told herself. But there, the anger. A tongue against a cut lip, she ponders it in the sallow light of the bathroom.

She wants to shove him. Maybe hit him with a rolled up magazine. Or suffocate him with a pillow. Good thing they lock the sleep lab, because if she saw him sleeping right now she might beat him awake and then senseless again. Whenever they'd fight he'd invariably fall asleep soon after, leaving her angry while he slept, slack jawed. She was pretty certain if he'd stayed she'd have eventually murdered him in his sleep.

She buys a bag of Smarties in the vending machine and desperately crunches them between her teeth. She hardly tastes them. It's the crushing she wants. And maybe that fake tasting waxy chocolate will slip some caffeine into her. She sits on one of the hard chairs in the lounge, her legs crossed, her dangling left foot bobbing. She grits her teeth against an infinite boredom with an acid edge of hurt. Two more sleep sessions to go. Maybe she can stay awake for the next two. If she stays this angry she is pretty sure it won't be a problem. She feels bad for being short with Saul. It wasn't his fault. She's the pervert who can't sleep unless there's someone to watch her sleep. That was the problem with him when they dated. He was always asleep. She would lie there watching him in the deep down under, in the sleepy deep, and she would feel such clear water envy.

She could never wake him either. A murderer could break into the house, stand on the foot of their bed and swing an axe at her and he wouldn't wake up. She pictured her blood splattered all over their sheets, all over his sleeping face. He might half swat away a splatter like a bad thought in his sleep. He might even roll away. But he wouldn't wake up even to hear her last breaths, wouldn't make any last declarations as she shuddered and sank away.

She needs to hold onto this anger for her next sleep session. She needs to stay awake. Having someone watch over her can't be the only solution to her insomnia. It just simply can't. She has tried most things: chamomile tea, warm milk before bed, cut out caffeine, no chocolate, even bought expensive sheets and listened to calming dolphin noises, though truth be told she finds whale and dolphin noises more depressing than relaxing. They sound so forlorn, calling out into the darkness. Plaintive cries, wailing whales. The stuff of nightmares or, worse, the stuff of lying in the dark, staring at the ceiling, called to, but unable to call back. She found one CD that was all water noises, creek water, waves on the beach. But things here are wet enough, she thought. Weeks with rain. Rain probably falls out there right now, but she can't see any-thing from within the sleep clinic. Odd. Like they want to deprive them of reality. It could even be night and she wouldn't know. That makes more sense, she guesses, that they want to divorce her internal clock from the real world. Timing is everything.

Half an hour left. Will he say sweet dreams again? Should she try and beat him to it. Should she hide in the washroom until he's come out and gone to the washroom himself, assuming he'll have to go after his sleep session? Then she could sneak into the sleep lab, avoid him altogether. He wouldn't see the anger on her face, wouldn't be able to get the first and last word in, and she could lie down on that bed . . . and, probably, promptly fall asleep.

**HE THINKS HE DOZED OFF** for the last fifteen minutes. He's not sure. The only clock hangs in the hallway. He thinks he slept for about fifteen minutes though. Not bad. He's a little pissed, but how much could they tell from fifteen minutes. And who wouldn't fall asleep after lying in a bed for over an hour and a half. Fifteen minutes, but maybe more.

He's mulling this over as he opens the sleep lab door and turns down the hallway. The hall glares linoleum and fluorescent without her. He shuffles towards the vending machines but the hard wooden chairs sit empty, lined up, bored with one another. Maybe she's finished her tests, scrammed home. She could be sleeping right now. Maybe after he left her she took to sleeping, got caught up on all that she had missed. The whole time he was in Mexico she slept, cocooned in their bed. In her bed. She wrapped up in the sheets and coma slept all those months. They would have gotten along so much better if she just slept more.

I can sleep tonight he tells himself. How many more sessions to get through? Two or three? He can't remember. Being awake nicks and cuts away at him, a slow torture. Maybe he does have narcolepsy. No, he really just loves sleep. He does love sleeping. He remembers a summer when he was twenty-one when all he did was work four hours a day at the bookstore down the road from his parents' house and then go home for a nap. Then play a few video games, fall asleep early, sleep late. He was drowning in sleep that summer. It feels hazy even in his memory. But a happy kind of hazy, blurry at the edges and sun worn. Oh to have that much sleep. Maybe he could take some time off work, the next few days, and just sleep when he gets home. Lately he doesn't feel like he can ever get caught up. Rested seems to elude him.

He slumps in one of the wooden chairs in the lounge. Yeah, a couple days off work. Close all the blinds. Stock up on microwavable foods, plastic trays of macaroni, pizza pockets, so he can just get up to eat, then crash again. Just sleep the days away, storing up again. Or he could even order in. Head lolling off to the side, the back of the chair digging into this shoulder blade, he suddenly slips asleep. He dreams he's being stabbed in the back. Literal dreams waste dreamtime. But she hovers on the edge of the dream. She has no shoes on. He doesn't know why he notices this. A younger her, younger than any version he has known; a glimpse of the woman before he helped her get all tied up in her expectations. And a plain oatmeal brown sugar kind of happy surrounds her. Not joyous, but hints of it in the corners of her eyes. The plain kinds of happiness often get overlooked.

**SHE FEELS SAD**. A sadness that clocks her before she can see it swing towards her. She'd had a plan. She waited in the washroom, combing her hair from her eyes, tilting her chin up to see her mouth better, reapplied lip balm, waiting for the sound of him going into the washroom so she could leave the women's washroom and walk down to the sleep clinic unscathed like he'd never been here at all. And then she heard him, heard the men's room door close and lock. She straightened her sweatshirt, exited the bathroom, and ran into him sleeping in the lounge, his head lolling back. It must have been the sleep lab technician who went into the washroom. She hadn't planned on that.

And how the hell did he manage to leave his sleep lab, get to the lounge, and fall asleep in the four or five minutes she was in the washroom. She doesn't need to remember now, how he looks sleeping. Sure, he's sitting up in an awkward wooden chair, but he sleeps the same way vertically as he does horizontally: head lolling, mouth wide open, so utterly unconscious, an unhinged bliss. She feels a pang and has to sit down, slump into the chair opposite him. She can't stop staring at his open mouth, the rise and fall of his breath. And she can't separate her longing for him now and her longing for sleep.

In his lap, a kid's magazine rests back cover up with an un-completed labyrinth puzzle. Ariadne gave Theseus the thread to go into the maze. She remembers a teacher explaining how Theseus found his way back. And she remembers thinking the teacher didn't really understand, how for Ariadne it meant she never had to let go of him, no matter how deep into the maze he went.

She hears the door to the men's room open, and then the attendant is standing in the hall beside the lounge. He puts his hands on his hips, less an attempt at a pose than a resting way he has about him. "He's asleep again."

"Still," she says.

The attendant laughs, an anxious heartiness to it like he knows it's inappropriate to laugh at patients.

"Shall we?" he asks.

"Yes," she says. She stands.

He pushes open the lab door with his right arm and gestures for her to go first, and he's doing that thing, where he attends to her so intently she wants to fall asleep right there where she's standing. Sleepwalk beside him wherever he might go.

# THE
# BEAUTIFUL
# DROWNED

# THE BEAUTIFUL DROWNED

**THE BODIES OF FISHERMEN** all wash up on this beach eventually. The restless bare beach near Inverness, naked facing north, the currents still washing up glass Japanese fishing floats. Sand bare, chilled, pressed smooth like a tablecloth by the sea's hands. Widows collect their drowned husbands on this beach. The trees bend away from the water, lean away with grief and yearning.

Cora finds them. She lines up the bodies of these drowned sailors, one two three, sometimes maybe even four, in a row, perpendicular to the waves to distinguish them from driftwood. Cora who wears three black dresses, and three black cloaks, all layered to keep the cold out, stained wet to her thighs by the lick of the waves, dragging torn strands of seaweed. Her bare feet, always bare on the sand, her footprints relaxing, giving up after a few breaths.

Boats betray their men. They crash against rocks, throw fishermen's bodies to the waves and jagged certainty. They tip over, trapping the fishermen hapless, unable to get to air. They stagger under bellies of fish and sink breathless as stones. Even out of water the boats kill the fishermen who crew them: they slip off winches and crush ribcages and spines, they tip in dry dock and pop skulls as easily as boots crush bulbs of bullwhip kelp. And still the men climb aboard, untie the lines, push off into the early morning light, plain as habit.

LILLY CAN'T REMEMBER when she first knew her husband would end up washed up on the beach of lost things. Maybe a year ago. Maybe after that bad spring storm. Or maybe after he didn't come home for two nights, a generous whore or the charity of a free bottle of whisky. He is simple and defined by such random kindnesses. So now, a year later, the nights he doesn't come home, she takes a lantern from the shed and winds down past the cannery row, past the Japanese wives tending fires in amongst the timbers and pilings, drying seaweed and salt pink salmon flesh, stirring their woks and pots. They watch her pass, calling their children to their skirts. They think she's a ghost, no other way to explain this recurring walk down to the water, her still silence like cold tongues lick up the backs of their necks, making them stir the soup a little faster.

The beach lies just up past cannery row, the inlet where the rapids between the village and the island throw flotsam up on the bedraggled shore. Fishermen know anything lost overboard that doesn't readily sink will wash up on this beach eventually. Only a matter of time and tide and the discretion of Cora.

Lilly says little to Cora. She brings her a small thermos of tea and she sits with her on the skeletal driftwood. She admires Cora's white translucence, a cold blue web of veins below her skin, the clear complexion of the drowned. She wonders what brought Cora here. The gossipy canning line carps say she was once one of them. But now Cora paces this length of beach, a rake made from driftwood wound together using cedar bark strips, she drags its teeth through the seaweed, the tide line, salvaging. The villagers who come looking for lost things always bring a gift, smoked salmon, maybe a halibut casserole, the seaweed crackers their dirty-cheeked children crunch, or, like Lilly, a thermos of tea, something to bring even a touch of colour to that woman's beluga white skin, slick in the mist.

At least once a week for months now, Lilly draws a blanket over her head and around her shoulders as a hood, the thermos under one arm, and sets out through the cedars, crosses the plank bridge over the sewage ditch, past the bored and idle stray dogs, down past little Japan and the old burnt cannery, the lonely pilings, the dull smooth glass bits flung across the rocks as stained glass, a meditation, a prayer to the abandoned.

Through the sea mist drowning the air, she can already see Cora, her slow plowshare pacing of the beach, stooping slow to drag fingers and the rake through sand and seaweed, to inspect the seaweed tide line, then rising again, her slow funeral procession languishing on. Behind the mist scrim, tidewaters retreated, the waves wash fast and thin across the long beach, layers and layers of modest skirts.

Lilly doesn't go to her, just finds the driftwood log, the large seat-height piece near Cora's fire, and waits, the salt mist raining down, the raspy rush of the waves after waves crashing over one another to sprawl on the sand. Cora will return to the fire, her pale drowned face and fingers peeking from the damp black garments in the firelight. Lilly waits listening to the rain tinkle across the beach rocks, down to the hiss of drops on the plain face of the sand. These sounds are Cora's.

Lilly can't see a shelter or a place where Cora might sleep. Maybe Cora just paces this beach, ceaselessly tracking across the sand, footprints washing away. If she slept, she might cease to exist, her waterlogged flesh collapsing like a jellyfish on sand. She must keep on moving. Or suffocate, gulping shudder and froth, in the open sea air.

Lilly shakes from the cold. Wants tea, but the first cup must be for Cora. Each night she comes here, she imagines what if it's tonight. What if he really did fall overboard, or the boat ran into the cable between a tug and its barge, slicing itself in two, and sank swiftly, or a rogue wave took them down faster than they could swallow. And what if he did wash up here? She sits on the log about six feet from the fire. The key is to be close enough to Cora to hear her murmurs without being so close that you can smell her, the fish-head rot and decay, the sea lice in the kelp, the cold wash and salt loss of her.

Cora, they say, like all monstrous women, had a threatening beauty once. Her father was Japanese and her mother was from the Tlingit tribe over on Lelu Island. Her mother didn't want to live in little Japan and her father didn't want to live in the shanty shacks, so they lived on the edge of each, on the last road that skirted the village. Her mother weathered the stares from the Japanese fishwives, the way they whispered to one another. And her father endured the shanty women's stares, how they whispered about the softness of his skin and rumoured that he smelled like almonds. Cora grew up there between the villagers' suspicions and their disquiet, lucky that despite all this her parents held hands on Sundays listening to plays on the radio, her father kissed her mother on the back of the neck at the stove, and she, in return, kissed him on the crown of his head at the table with his Archie comics. They lived in the in-between, but most schoolyards, she found, like most villages don't like in-betweens. The Japanese girls felt she was common, dirty. The Tlingit boys regarded her as exotic. Both assumed she was easy. None of the girls would play with her anyway, so she might as well play with the boys.

That was decades before they exiled her though. Long before her father drowned and her mother hanged herself in the bathroom, worn nylons and a sturdy shower rod.

**LILLY WONDERS WHAT** Cora does with drowned fishermen. Is she gentle with them, does she stroke their bare bloated faces, does she comb their hair into place, preparing for the loved ones who might come looking? Does she search their pockets for spare change, keys to things they'll no longer open, sodden photographs of people they will no longer love? And does she keep these things, thinking to herself that some lost things are best kept lost?

Lilly likes to think about him, drowned seawater dribbling from his slack mouth, how this mad woman, this Cora, might find him, draw his jaw closed, holding it there until rigor mortis sets in, perhaps kissing his closed mouth to seal it. After the drowning, the sea tumbled flailing, the pummel and spew to shore, her hands, her kiss will reassure him the sea green vagaries have passed. Reassure him that Lilly will come to collect him, put him in the ground behind the village where he can look down the hill at the whitecaps on the bay, warm in the graveyard's soft, muskeg bed with the beetles and the watchful arms of the cedars.

This is what Lilly and the other villagers ask of Cora, the woman they exiled to this beach, remote from their husbands. Only to hope their drowned fishermen husbands — because all fisherman drown sooner or later — will wash back to her, so her hands can drag them from the surf, her kiss can salvage them on this strand. The village women abandon jealousy, for their men are dead and she is no longer a woman. A ferryman, an undertaker, she belongs to the fathoms and the crustaceans.

When he drowns, Cora will know him by his jaw. Wider than his neck, Lilly heard her younger sister giggling with her friends, calling him a sea bass. Her cheek nuzzled against the itchy warm fur of his chest, she would gaze with longing at the jut of that jaw. She has a narrow head, far more narrow than his. Thinks they must look like an odd vowel pair, a 'u' and an 'i.' She likes how this jaw, his muscular neck rides above her, almost beastly, torquing to the side. He does not look at her. She tried, tried climbing on top of him, tried grabbing that jaw in her hands, ached to be face to face in the gap-toothed shanty shack, his cold thick bottom lip between hers. But he would look up and away to the corner of the room, avoid her eyes, sometimes brace his forearm across her neck and the side of her torqued head, force her to look away, so all she covets now are his vein muscled neck, that deep water bass jaw. Covets and half hopes he will fall overboard and wash up so she can grieve or feel anything other than this keelhaul longing.

Cora drops her rake as she paces up towards the fire and Lilly. She doesn't acknowledge Lilly, does not call out a hello, but strides to the beached tree, shadows the other end. She must know why Lilly is there, as it's always the same reason. But she always leaves Lilly waiting. But then waiting means nothing to Cora. Means nothing like tea or fire or rain might. So Lilly watches the fire and waits.

The wind picks up, buffeting them there on the log. Cora turns to Lilly, slightly, her cheeks visible in the folds of the blankets drawn around her. Lilly unscrews the lid of the thermos, then the cap, then pours the steaming tea into the lid, half full, handing it across the distance between them. Cora nods slightly then, reaches for the tea. As she passes the cup, Lilly feels Cora's cold, wet fingers on hers, looks down to hide her own flash of disgust.

The two women lean into the salted wind off the water, various stages of silence, the hot tea between them, the fire crackling. Rain hisses the sand and then ebbs away to the sound of the waves sluicing the shore, and then Lilly asks the small question she's come to ask.

"Is he here?"

The slow shake of Cora's head.

**AS THEY THRONGED** outside her house, Cora must have thought about fighting them, those nasty canning-line wives. She never seduced any man, none of their husbands. The men came to her, came to that house with smoked salmon, with salmon pickled in jars, with gobs of shrimp in newspaper and plastic bags, with moonshine in canning jars and sometimes the good ones even with beef, though most people in the village only ate beef once or twice a year. She liked beef, and she liked the men who would bring it. They sometimes hesitated after they handed it over, a couple of steaks wrapped in brown butcher paper. Hesitant like they sort of hoped she would sear those steaks for them. Like they might get up under her dress and have her feed them after. Maybe they didn't desire this, but she liked thinking she disappointed them, that she sent them home with a little hunger as she slipped her dress back on.

Phone lines were slow to come to the village because canning lines are more effective. The Japanese women gut the fishes in a flurry of knives, the Native women hosing the blood and innards away sort the fish, the Italian women in a flurry of hands patch and weigh the cans that need more flesh. Each group has an informal translator, a woman who can speak a little English. The Japanese woman who can speak a little English speaks to the Italian woman who can speak a little English who speaks to the Native woman who can speak enough English, and this way town meetings are held up and down the canning lines. Italian women from the trailer park, Native women from the reserve houses at the end of the road, the Irish and Ukrainian shanty women and Japanese women from little Japan all work on a machine line and its sole purpose is to bring metal and fish together so it can be consumed elsewhere.

The few men who move among these women, who grease these machines and untwist them when they clinch up and break down, they know to just dart in and out with grease guns and wrenches and then retreat to the millwright's shop at the back wall. A sanctuary where they hide, take turns napping to the clanking rhythm of the canning lines, soothed into ignoring the rattling gossip underneath the machine noise. Posters and calendars of big-breasted naked blond women watch over them, this cannery, like guardian angels of the impossible possible.

Lilly knows that Cora knows who her husband is. The other women told her how they'd seen him stagger to her place, his swagger stagger they called it. He's one of those men who women find sexy when he's drunk, the boyish round mouth, the sea bass jaw, the curly black hair. She's seen the way the other women look at him, even as they are telling tales about how he used to stagger down to the shacks, the last row of shacks before little Japan and the cannery. How he would fall into Cora, give her those scraps of him, the messy bilge love. But if Lilly spent her time being angry, carrying wrath for the women he had washed up on, she'd never talk to another woman in this sad, septic village.

She knew the moment she met him, in her father's corner store, that she wanted to be his wife, wanted to have him in a way all these crotch-watching, thigh-gnawed cannery line whores could never have him. She even thought he might change, the way fishermen's wives think their husbands might change. But all the mythologies her mother read her as a child were right: women are changeable, not the men. She said yes to him because she couldn't see then that he would change her from a wife to a woman waiting, waiting for her husband to drown and let her at last become a widow.

And with that simple sway of her downturned head, with that small gesture of no, Cora pushes herself up from the log, raises the cup in her hands to her lips where she blows on it, the steam billowing out towards the water, and she sips. She only ever takes one sip. The halibut belly white of Cora's cheeks stain the slightest blush deep down, a bare glimpse before she turns towards the water, returns to her slow seaweed and broken shell parade, one hand lifting her skirts as she goes. The rain falls harder, hissing on the sand and filling the space between the two women. Maybe after all Lilly's waiting, this woman now too wonders when he will wash up, limp limbed, mouth agape, and colder than even her.

Nakashima's wife, they say, the one with the gourd-round face and thin weed of a mouth started the long canning line conversation. Truly, none of this would ever have happened if Nakashima hadn't snuck up onto Cora's back porch with those dumplings. None of the Japanese men had ever visited Cora. Not that they had a more fervent sense of morality, they just feared their wives more, for only the Japanese women wielded knives on the canning lines.

But Nakashima saved the dumplings his wife had made for him, and that afternoon, after they emptied out the belly of his fishing boat, he walked the back road up from the water, all the way up to Cora's house, to stand on her porch with dumplings. No one had ever brought her dumplings, so she was intrigued. She wondered how it would feel to run her hands up his smooth back, inhale the scent at the nape of his torqued neck, taste the tideline where his leg met his abdomen.

As a child, she had wondered if her father smelled different than other men. Wondered if he even smelled different than other Japanese men, because her mother didn't cook Japanese the way the wives down in little Japan did. Cora's mother would, sometimes, cook potato pancakes for him, but she liked her potatoes. And potato pancakes are more Korean than Japanese, but Cora didn't know that then. Only years later, long after she'd been shunned and run out, would a Korean family move to town.

And, when the father's boat went down off the lighthouse, they brought her potato pancake, explained it was Korean. Told her that before they carried away their father's waterlogged, battered body. They didn't notice that his hair was combed, that his clothes were dry. Cora had never seen a Korean man naked before.

Nakashima, anxious, climbed on top, then wriggled under her like he was trying to play out several fantasies in one afternoon. But the dumplings were tasty. A little harsh, slightly overcooked and heavy on the rice vinegar, like his wife's mouth. But she couldn't help wonder, why today? Why did he wake up today, decide to save the dumplings and set about coming to see her?

TUESDAY, the sheriff tells her he caught her husband up against the monkey bars at the school playground around midnight with a woman the sheriff wouldn't name. Thursday, Mrs. Anders corners her at the corner store to demand she keep her husband from peeing in her yard. A yard requires grass, not just a tree stump and packed dirt with mounds of pine needles. But by Sunday she has gone three days with no reports of him and the wind rushes the cedar branches and tears the whitecaps on the bay. Near dusk, she steeps black tea in the thermos, stockings herself with her husband's long underwear, coils shawls and scarves around her shoulders and neck to hold back the wind, then funeral waltzes along the muddy and mossy path, past the women who whisper about her husband. The shack wives' faces, loathing her morbid vigil, fearing she might wish their husbands down into the depths with hers. They don't understand the pleasure she finds in imagining his sodden, bloated body floating out there in the straits, barnacles latching on, their tongues fluttering out from him as he undulates in the currents, hundreds of hungry mouths buffeted and slowly sinking down with him.

A widow, she could mourn then, at last. More pity, less shame. And all the stories would be old stories, no new ones she didn't know yet, all his new tricks and stumbles from the night before, the fist fights with husbands who found him with their wives, the screaming wives who sometimes found him with their husbands, the solitary ones who had no one to betray except themselves. She didn't know what to do with so many stories.

Halfway to the water, as she crosses the board bridge, she hears his laugh. Four shacks down. She follows his raven caw laughter through the cedar and spruce vigilant and hushing in the wind. A widow's shack. The woman with the hooked nose and the wide buttocks, one of the ones who won't speak to Lilly, who blame her for her husband's lasciviousness, and pity her from a gossipy distance in case her weakness might be as contagious as fish lice.

Yes, his laugh, a tumult of memories of his laugh, his cheek against her belly, his belly against her back in those first nights together, a few sober days in their kitchen, his hands on her hips, snuffling the nape of her neck while she cut celery at the counter, her kissing the back of his neck as he tied flies at the kitchen table. She didn't know she should be collecting up the laugh and sealing it in sterilized jars to keep for all the cold linoleum nights. That laugh now cackles out of the clapboard and across the roofs. That widow must have gotten over her grief. Women as musical chairs, with no music and no chairs.

She veers north for the beach. She longs to see Cora's pale flesh, its smooth cockleshell white, wishes her culled heart wouldn't stain her skin so readily. Maybe tonight she will ask Cora if she has found something else for her. A watch. A lost dress flung up like a deflated octopus. A seagull's wing encrusted with bottle worms. Or maybe she will just ask after other drowned fishermen. She could claim someone else's drowned fisherman as her own. Have his body carried back to the shacks, lay him on the dining room table, remove his sea soaked clothes, soap the salt from him with kitchen cloths, fall on his bare chest and wail her grief, dress him in her husband's navy blue wedding suit. Her husband is a stranger now, anyway, why shouldn't a stranger become her husband. A man who could benefit from her inconsolable wailing. Maybe a strange man, the kind who never knew women. Never kissed or scraped his beard along the bare soft length of a woman's neck. She thinks about what it would be like to undress a stranger. The only man she's ever seen naked is her husband. And his nakedness never left any room for her. She could give the gentle goodbye this drowned bachelor fisherman deserves.

**COINCIDENCE SLIPPED IN** off the water with the fog that day. If Nakashima's wife hadn't been walking the tree line back up to the swamp foraging for mushrooms — some ink caps, some jelly ears — and hadn't seen the banana leaves she had wrapped the dumplings in, empty and discarded in Cora's trash can out back where the raccoons had knocked it over, maybe none of it would have happened. For her husband to sleep with that half-breed was one thing. For him to give her dumplings to that woman was quite another.

So Nakashima's wife brought her anger to work that day, and for the first time one of the Japanese canning line women spoke of husbands and that Cora woman, hollered about her over the clatter clanging of the canning lines. They rarely spoke to the Italians. The Italians had been ready for this conversation long ago. Of the six Italian women, five of them had husbands who had taken their pastas to see Cora more than once. Only two of them cared. The other three admitted relief that their husbands took their greasy, hairy asses to bother someone else. And the

Native women, well, they never liked her but they didn't like her because her Japanese father had given her those cheek bones that always made her look like she thought she was a little superior and their men thought so too. But that said, the woman Cora and her ways now tempting and courting the Japanese men gave the women's various angers a single, indecent, consolidating target.

So the Japanese women, cutting fish flesh with their flurry knives, cried the injustice back and forth over the cacophony of the canning line, pinballing off one another until they were angry enough, then passed the story to the Italian women, who passed it to the Native women, and it was Harriet Henry, the oldest of the Native women who said to the others, "I haven't even tried Nakashima's dumplings." And translated from Tlingit to English to Italian to English to Japanese, her complaint became a dirge of canning line women's cries to set fire to the whore's house and immolate her in it. And this might have remained mere blowfish talk had Nakashima's wife not looked at her watch and said simply "5:00!" Most of their husbands wouldn't be home for dinner until 6:30. They could burn the place, run her off and be back in time to make a simple dish, pasta and cheese in the trailer park, hamburgers in the shanty, and rice and fish for cannery row. So the time of the culling passed the other way down the canning line. And the women nodded, turned back to their sharp-rimmed cans and pink salmon flesh with excitement, though some said later they didn't think they were really going to do it. Thought it was just talk.


**THE NEXT SUNDAY**, seven days since her last vigil, Lilly staggers, slips on the slick wood planks of the boardwalk, winding her way back to the beach. She already worked a full day at the convenience store, feet mashed in sneakers flattening on the concrete.

Now her weary cortege to the beach, past little Japan, up the bluff, past the last cannery, around the peninsula, and up to the crest and its little cliff looking over the open ocean. She hears the groans even above the wind and the waves on the rocks below. And there he is, his white naked ass a grotesque mushroom in among the tree roots, rising and thrusting, a woman's legs spread awkward shaking branches either side of him. Scramble of legs, her bare feet on gravel as she pushes out from under him and stumbles, falls to grab clothes, covering herself before the second rock hits the gravel next to them, Lilly reaching down for a larger one. She'd so expected she was going to be a widow, but instead she's just a stupid girl with this skinny white assed, stray dog, poor lay of a man wailing, blurry drunk with his little erection, angry red rhubarb nub in spring.

The groans were his, after all, the woman was making none. Lilly recognizes her, Tanya, the elementary school secretary who moved to the village just the year before. She skids on the rocky path, tugging her panties up, "I'm so sorry, I don't do this kind of thing, I just," and then she saw the larger rock in Lilly's hand and took off on a limping retreat across the jagged rocks and pebbles of the path, her shirt and then a sock falling to the ground, but she didn't turn back.

"Come back!" he bellows after the secretary, his pants around his ankles, staggering as he tries to stand. "You fucking ruined it," he sneers as he reaches down to pull up his pants.

At first she's startled, thinks someone else has thrown the rock that ricochets off his forehead with a thud and crack as though it has found some way to split his dense-boned forehead. She wouldn't. But she looks down at her empty hand, a few specks of dirt, feels the burn of shoulder muscle. She threw it. But even as he falters backwards, tripping on the pants around his ankles, on the brink of the cliff, she does not feel bad, does not call out.

Instead, her breath hitches in her lungs, lips part, gust of salt and rain off the water crests the cliff, blinds her so she clenches her eyes shut.

Gone. The wide blue-grey ocean, livid and steely, now uninterrupted between the cedars and spruce. Whitecaps on the straits, sharp as little white knives. If she could control the weather she would make whitecaps all the time.

**AT 5:00**, women roiled from the shanties, down from the trailer park on the hill, and up from the cannery row, clutching their own boxes of matches and a few, the ones crying out, their lurid shouts echoing up the treetops of the mountainside behind the village, with gas cans they stole from husbands' skiffs or storage shacks. Reaching Cora's shack, they clumped together whispering, bulging against some invisible wall.

Cora peeked through the glaucous curtains, her belly and chest exhaling relief. They had come at last. She just didn't know it would take dumplings. She would have rather had beef. She could not decide whether to fight back, so she turned on the television, idly following a soap opera she never watched, occasionally peeking out the curtains.

The less angry women, when the lynching and immolation didn't immediately materialize, took to chatting, odd peals of laughter running under the angry women's shouts. Here and there in the crowd, some took turns checking their watches. Most had to be home by 6:00 to make dinner and they began to doubt the resolution of the others, suspect that there might be no spectacle after all.

By 5:45 it was either torch the shack or resign themselves to husbands who make them fools. By 5:45 Nakashima's wife and the Mancuso woman, the one whose husband could be seen coy on Cora's back stoop with his wife's pastitsio at least once a week, decided that even if all the other women cowered home, they each had to hurl fire or just continue dying. Mancuso snatched the bottle of gas one of the other Italian women had brought, lit the rag hanging from it; Nakashima's wife grabbed the whole tank of gas she herself had brought and unscrewed the cap. She spun in a circle like a discus thrower and hurled the red plastic tank up on the porch where it thumped and skidded, spraying gas just as the Mancuso woman's bottle with the fiery rag shattered on the boards, a wave of flames splashing over the wood deck and walls, then exploding the red plastic tank, startling and shellshocking the gangs of women to stumble back, trip, and fall in a jumble on the ground. A wave of gasps among the women, and then cheers. Then a small shudder of worry as the woman named Cora, that whore, did not emerge and the flames tore up the roof and the heat from the flames exploded the windows.

**LILLY EDGES CLOSER** to the cliff, scanning the rocky tide pools below for him. He's sprawled, a leg broken out to the side like it's pointing to some other option she can't see from here. He's probably still alive. If the tide were in, he might drown in his unconscious state. She could run back to the village, tell the constable. A group of men would come back here, they would pull up his pants. They would carry him back up to the village, or at least to the first cannery where they could administer first aid. He might not remember. And even if he did, maybe he would at last fear her a little. But then she would have to care for him, carry the burden of his brokenness. She could tell the other wives about Tanya, the secretary, and she would be jobless, exiled. Some jagged pleasure in that.

Climbing down to the rocky beach, she slips on the moss and rocks. Ahead, his head lolls back and forth in agony. Maybe she could apologize for throwing the rock, and maybe he'd hit her. Even things up, he'd say. The whitecaps, the bullwhip kelp in the surges. If he blacks out, he could easily drown. It wouldn't be like she'd killed him, the rock, the fall, the tide, the pretty whitecaps smiling.

**THE NIGHT** the cannery women set fire to Cora's house, sagging on the edge of the evergreens and the moss, some of them thought she would choose to sacrifice herself to the flames, consumed with her own guilt. But inside, Cora ran through the house. She grabbed her mother's winter jacket, a blanket, and her father's scarf, while outside the screams and cheers of the women surged. Quick panic shot down her neck so she ran out the back door, barefoot through the moss. Three of the Italians saw her and let out a cry. All the women swarmed after her then, throwing the gas and matches they had brought on the fire, some hobbling, chugging their arms, others agile but soon into the chase gasping bent over propped on their thighs; nothing in the village had ever demanded this urgency. Cora turned away then, ran with every follicle, with every ounce of muscle; lungs blasting with rhythmic gasps as she plunged down the tree line, bare feet on moss and muskeg. She refused to let these women's teeth and nails tear her to pieces.

Nakashima and Mancuso had started the chase, but four or five younger, more agile women like the Maracle wife, the one whose husband had more beautiful hair than Cora, were yards ahead of the two instigators. The women's faces contorted, twisted and vivid with all the small angers cresting into howls for what Cora had done, yes, but also just for the fearful waiting, the longing, the feral-teethed children, the sad particulars of being a fisherman's wife. Cora must pay for it all until she'd be nothing more than pieces of flesh for the canning line.

She hurled down the tree line to the main road, past the schoolyard, through the park, down to cannery row, the other women flagging, some walking the chase, still resolved though the distance between her and them expanded. The men prairie dogged out of the bar, out of the mechanic's shop next door, saw their women, heard their screams, retreated, gulping beer, peering through the shuttered windows silent, cowering, melancholy that Cora was the one the women chased. When the screams simmered down, they sat back on the bar stools with their beers, debating whether going home early tonight or very late would be safer.

Cora sprinted out of cannery row and then hurtled herself up the mossy, grassy bluff above the rocky beach. Maybe thirty yards between her and the wives in the lead, her face broke open with hope, her knees knifing higher up the hill. If she had to run to Alaska, run to the Arctic, and across the ice fields to Russia, she would outrun these women.

At the last outposts of the village, the wives gasped for breath, glancing back and at their watches, shaking their heads, remembering they still had to make dinner, despite the hunt. Nakashima's wife and the Mancuso wife both hollered for the chase to continue, stamina fading as they huffed, up the rocky path, distance building between them and the other wives who staggered to a stop, talking among each other, one saying to some others, "Well she's got no house to fuck in now. Problem solved."

**LILLY CLINGS TO** the half-submerged rock ledge where he lies broken, the seaweed and algae covered rocks ready to betray her. She wants to say he was broken before she ever touched him. His agony face, the blood on the rocks below his head, the leg at a right angle. She grabs him by the arm, heaves him up, drags him a few feet and then drops him. His head cracks down on the rock and he cries out. She lifts and heaves again. She imagines it will take ten or so tries, but the tide's rising, she's up to her waist and the waves help her lift, as she pulls him, slipping a little on the seaweed strewn rocks, but his body begins to float, launched. She floats him around so her back is to the shore, and then with all her weight she pushes him out, his head dunking underwater for a moment, so he surfaces choking, then a whimper. His limbs struggle weakly and he can't swim or tread water with his leg like that.

His hair sops to his forehead. She remembers the first time he came back from a week out at sea, he and the other men staggering up the hill from the docks haunted from lack of sleep, blue from the frigid sea heaving itself over them. He floated on his side in their tub, warm water pinking his limbs, head lolling against the porcelain lip unconscious. As he drowsed she slowly added kettles of boiling water, stirring the hot into the warm, swirling currents around his naked skin with her bare hands, brushing his flanks, a strawberry stain blushing up her neck.

A wave surges her feet off the rocks, rests her down again. With the rhythm of breaths, the ocean lifts her, weightless, then exhales her feet to the seaweed and barnacle dressed rocks. He sinks down then buoys up sputtering, another whimper. Her teeth clack together with the cold. He submerges under the next wave and she can't see him. No bubbles as the bottle green waves surge and drag him further out. She buffets in the surges.

He doesn't surface again. She imagines him in the diminishing murky light, balletic and listing downward, barnacles, limpets, and muscles bejeweling him, a crust of hunger and thirst.

**THEY SAY THE NIGHT** of the burning Cora knew the cannery women had stopped chasing her, but she didn't give up running. She scrambled over the bluff, hands clawing in the muskeg to get past the steep face of it, past the peninsula, down to the beach where the rapids and the whitecaps swelled and threw flotsam up on the sand. The only sandy beach on the north coast, but it lay shunned by the villagers because the sea coughed up corpses, flotsam, and detritus there. The beach backed up against a steep mountain at the armpit between the island and the mainland so clouds crowded against one another, a sopping mass of mist and rain even on the rare day the village had sun.

Cora, staggering, fell onto the beach, on all fours struggling, her bleeding, torn feet burning on the cold, salt-washed sand. Her breath heaving, she flung off the blanket, the jacket, the scarf, abandoning them on the sand. The rain pelted her skin, splashing her face, washing her chill and bare. Her skin paled whiter in that blue light. Her mother's colour, her father's colour, both bled out of her into the sand. She was now whiter than the trailer park Irish, the shantytown white trash. She sunk to the sand, a ghost fish beached there, thrown up from the sea trench depths.

The waves buffeted her further up the beach, stranded her, frothed around her again. She had used every muscle, every breath to escape the village women, and abandoned herself jetsam on the beach, the gulls and the eagles hovering in the winds off the water waiting. When the tide came to her for the third time, she chewed the rubbery seaweed tossed up around her, sluice of seawater gushing in her mouth. She crawled slower than the tides returned, up past the tideline into the beach shrubs and under the windblown cedars and there she found salal and cloud berries and the fever sleep of the Kodiaks in winter.

Then the night of the disaster of the *L'Amie*. The fishing boat bellying home, gut full, the slurry captain who didn't see the cable strung ahead of them between the tugboat and its barge, and, engines full, the boat rammed the cable, slicing itself in half, the sleeping crew's dreams taking on water, they only woke to drown, the skipper awake to feel his ship drag his crew to the sea bottom. Eight women woke up widows, mothers lost their sons, and after they wrapped themselves in black and gulped on their gumboots they clomped down to the beach at the end of the currents to search for the bodies of their drowned men. When they reached the long stretch of sand, their men were already there, lined up in peaceful rows of rest. Haunting the other end of the beach, paced Cora. They knew she had found their husbands and cared for their corpses. They also feared she might be the wrathful creature who would now pull fish boats down into the deep, drowning the helpless bastards. So they built her a fire, brought her food, old sweaters and overcoats, gifts to thank her for caring for their dead, insurance against future losses.

**THE WIND PRICKLES** Lilly's face with flung sand grains, waves tripping over one another to shore, the grey sea foaming at the tide line. Past a large fallen tree upturned by a storm, branches and roots stuck out in distress, Cora has circled him with a bed of seaweed and shells. Beauteous. The water has bloated him, taken the furrows and hollows out of his face and his eyes, his sea bass jaw fitting at last, washed up from the depths. His blue lips long to be kissed, his combed neat hair slicks his face into kindness. Cora has done all this for her. Lilly wants to embrace her, but tears are rushing down her cheeks, a wail bawling from her seized jaw. Cora stands vigil beside her, head bowed, a kindness that shucks Lilly's grief open so she falls to the frigid sand, her body crumpling in spasm, a creature hauled up from the depths too quickly. Ancient small griefs hitch up, retch out onto the sand, then retch forth more.

The tide leans in and steps back again before she rises, sand falling from her, wanders back up the beach, to the fire. She folds her rain slicker, stacks it with the thermos of tea, pot of stew and the bundle of biscuits on the log for Cora. Her cooking tastes plain compared to the dishes cooked by some of the other village women, not as tasty as Nakashima's wife's dumplings. But her stew and biscuits don't invite complications. She climbs back up to the village to retrieve the constable, to present him with her drowned husband. To find black clothes to wear. To become, at last, a widow.

# BEAUTIFULLY
## USELESS

# BEAUTIFULLY USELESS

**NOT HARD TO IMAGINE** a father who is absent; you can do it I am sure. Imagine he's absent, a handful of memories before you're seven, then gone for five years before he dies, without you, with relatives you don't know beside him. You could have been there. Your mother crumpling in the door to the living room, sandbagged with grief and the desire to protect you. Do you want to go, I'll take you, her voice fleeing across the floor to another room. Organ failure, unconscious, they say on the phone. He will have no words left. Even if he had all the words in his lap, the life still in him, what could he say to you that might fill over the cracks, the chasms of years without him.

Still, now as an adult, you have curiosity, might want to know where he went for those five years. Who he loved, who loved him back, whether, despite the trajectory of his disintegrating, plummeting wreckage of a life, he might have found small pockets of happiness. Something. You wouldn't begrudge him that.

You only have two pictures of him: one where he wears a goblin mask, holds you, tickling you, making you laugh (from a year before he left, you hold the photo under a magnifying glass trying to see if his expression, how he looks past you to another room, betrays signs of his imminent departure); the other with the two of you, picking seashells on the beach, his face grave like he's explaining something to you (two months after the divorce, a surprise visit, your mother standing at the top of the steps at home her hand over her mouth and nose, holding back, you realize now, the gutting of grief). Only two pictures, poor props to reconstitute a life, to understand the man you might want to understand.

Then imagine you found out from one of those relatives you don't know, one who tracks you down a decade later, that in your father's poverty, in his clumsy search for some kind of happiness, he was in a film once. An erotic film. And here's the question, the itchy question: would you watch the film?

It arrives in the mail. Even in this age of internet file sharing the only place you could find a copy was a mail order warehouse. It arrives five weeks after you ordered it, just on the night when you forgot it might arrive. How as soon as you forget it's possible to close your fingers in a car door, the door finds its moment to remind you. One of those nights the rain drenches you so all you can think about is being sopping wet. Or you are hungry beyond distraction, no food in sight. No matter, but you are not expecting the small, thick parcel in your mailbox, plain yet smug with its own importance. And you are in pain, or wet, or famished, but you are now face to face with a brown parcel like a letter bomb, and your mind stops communicating with your body for a moment, like that time you did a chin-up on a chin-up bar that wasn't properly attached to the door frame and you landed on your back on the threshold, the breath bashed from you. Just like that. An erotic video wrapped in brown paper, all that's left of your father.

You think maybe you could get someone else to watch this video, watch it and select the less Oedipal parts to watch. There must be interstitial scenes, moments without full porn. They could tell you what to watch and what not to watch. But you're caught wondering if it would be worse to imagine what your father did in the gaps this supposed friend censored. And, though it's perverse, you can't fathom letting someone, anyone, know your father more than you do. As small as this might be.

The parcel sits on the coffee table half malevolent, half embers consuming the air in the room, pulsing light, so you see Cheerios where they fell beside the couch, dust bunnies hunkered down licking themselves. There are a thousand things you could be doing besides staring at this parcel. So much cleaning you've put off, the broken shelf in the fridge, the crack in the bathroom window, the tear in the hall wallpaper, all need fixing, all come to mind in this moment as you stare at the parcel containing what remains of your father.

Someone wrapped it neatly, deliberately. Someone who should have a job at Christmas in a mall wrapping presents for those who are adhesive-tape challenged. You stare at the seams, wondering about these careful hands. A way to put off the opening.

You orbit other rooms, making the bed you forgot to make, sluicing and scrubbing fossilized dishes, flossing, resisting the parcel's gravitational pull. You can't think about the various kinds of destruction, the possible injuries that might come from watching the video. You think of family members who might be revolted, aghast that you even looked for this video, let alone ordered it, and then considered watching it on a Thursday night.

You whip up pasta, from dry noodles, a can of pureed tomatoes, and loads of parmesan to cover the fact that there's no meat or other vegetables in the pasta. You think you make good pasta, but you don't. No one has told you this because it's a small thing.

You eat the poor pasta in the kitchen, out of the line of sight of the parcel. You sense that you can't put this off much longer. You place your dishes in the sink. You don't remember eating the pasta. The pot steamed on the stove, then it was gone, the sauce-stained dishes in the sink, your stomach full. One less thing to think about. You remember you have half a bottle of Scotch in the cupboard above the fridge. This is one of those occasions where drinking alone is not only permissible but required.

You bang back one glass. The next you add ice cubes, thinking this might make you sip it. But you chug it back anyway, freezing your front teeth. And when your shoulders feel warm, you figure it's time. You don't want to be too drunk or too sober for this.

You run a fingernail along the adhesive tape seam, you break the paper free from itself, and underneath you find a VHS tape, no cover, merely a fresh label that says "College Guy #58." And you realize your father was just one of many guys who went to some fictional porn college. He never really went to real college. You know this. Or feel fairly certain. Letters at Christmas, phone calls on birthdays for the first couple years, his ideas for new businesses, plans for you to come visit maybe next summer. He was full of little hopes followed by little failures in predictable succession.

You have to dig out the VCR you store under a bolus of scarves and gloves in the top of the hall closet. You attach the VCR to the TV. You place the tape in the front of the deck and, holding your breath, you push the tape in. It clunks into place. Adjusts itself. Ready to play.

You decide to perhaps watch it on visual fast forward to begin. Maybe skate across the surface of the whole thing, blurring your eyes even, so you might map out the most traumatizing stuff first.

You press play, then fast forward. Images of him begin to streak by. Look how young he is. Was. You see him sitting on a couch, talking to the camera, he strips down, flexes, does pushups. Then he's outside, strips off his underwear, then jumps into the pool. Much splashing, much nakedness in water. Then he climbs out onto the deck. You realize this isn't a fetish video, that so far it seems like there won't be any sex with animals or feces involved, so you rewind to the place where he poses. You press play again. You watch him flex his biceps. He's in really good shape. He's your father and he's in really good shape. You think about him dying, his diseased body failing on a hospital bed, and this doesn't seem to match the body in the video, the muscular, healthy looking body.

He flexes, then he turns towards the camera, blushes, lowering his head, and maybe it's a gesture you have yourself made on occasion. Or maybe he has your hairline, the same gap in his front teeth or his nostrils flare in the same way. No matter, in this small moment you just see he really is your father. He has narrow hips. He looks so young, even younger than you are now.

You could be wrong, maybe you just want to believe this, need to believe this, but that fragile smile, the red blotches rising on his chest, the blush creeping into his cheeks all seem to say he hasn't done this before. And you've only heard of the one video. So that must be. You know that consoles you somehow. You'd rather not have to do this again, perhaps see a decline in him. You prefer this VHS memory now, this simple sun, chlorine-washed place before the wreckage.

He drops his track pants. You press fastforward.

He floats in the pool. Press play. He dunks under, his naked butt to the air, then surfaces, spits water like a toy rubber dolphin. This surprises you. You feared all kinds of things you might see, but didn't expect this moment, childlike, as though he is on a beach, his hair blonder than you remember, bleached from the sun and bare-foot running across the strand where he was six once and ran and ran, heaving small rib cage, to the salt water, to somersaults in the surf, to breathless air-breaking, chokes on the water, wiping from his face, wide perfect teeth smile. He was six once, you see. He wasn't always a father.

He rises out of the water at the pool's edge. His hair washed down his face, he tosses it back, a slight smile. He places his hand on the deck in front of him and pushes himself free of the water.

You see him again in all his nakedness. If you had a normal childhood, where he would have been around, you probably would have seen him naked before this. Dads bathe or shower with their kids. Are naked with them in pool change rooms. But you have never seen your father naked before tonight. He doesn't look like a father. And all you can think is that people must have desired him. Men and women must have wanted to see him naked. And maybe he even seems happier naked.

A close-up shot of his face, eyes closed, as he lies on the pool deck in the roaring sun, and you see you don't have his mouth. He has a downturned Rossetti mouth, lower lip thicker, more pulpy than the upper, and narrow. You got your mother's wide mouth, or her thin lips, or her closed-mouth smiles, but in any event, you didn't get his decadent, ripe mouth.

You see what your mother might have seen at a school dance, in boring half-mown front yards one summer, or maybe at the park pool, casual glances as he walked by on the concrete deck. Before she found out he liked men instead. Yet even that makes him more beautiful, somehow distant on a summer dock, looking off instead of at her, she can taste the moment he will turn to her. The way you watch him, his bottom lip jutting a little, his eyes closed, the sun loving him.

He rises to one elbow, swings around so he is crouching and springs up to stand, a grin preempted when the video cuts to a bedroom. Clad with only a bed and a lamp, the room blares fakery and he stands innocent, duped, as the characterless room threatens to erase him. You watch him lie down on the bed in shorts, with a pornographic magazine. You watch him lie down and you know what comes next, what only could come next. So you pause the video there. Anything that follows will mar this fuzzy VCR reverie.

You rewind the video to the flexing part again, then pause. The tape stands still with the image of him, back to the camera, biceps flexed, his head just beginning to turn towards you. This moment promises the next, the space between breaths. You sit on the couch in your living room, the torn brown paper on the coffee table in front of you. Your father's flexed back and biceps flickering on the television. The VHS must stand in for all the memories you do not have. He is not quite happy, it's true, more nervous than anything. But radiant. Unblemished.

The images shutter by in your memory, glaring the backs of your eyes. Like when you were five on the wide arched beach looking directly at the sun, bleaching the colours from the sand, the parasols, the waves around you. The glare of light swallows these celluloid flashes as the reel pulls those other images into its furnace, too: how you fear he might have looked in other rooms, strewn on gritty floor mattresses, longing; how you imagined he looked in the hospital bed, sick shadows smudging his lines, his body failing, but now, too, how he must have looked to someone who loved him, even for a moment, as he napped on a nuzzled bed, the gloam of the sun ebbing on the pool deck outside. This one image persists, his broad back flexed as he promises to turn to you, and you call this memory.

# HANDS

# HANDS

**A DAY MADE OF GLASS**. She feels it before she even pulls back the covers. Outside the kitchen window, the rain falls heavy and glaring, the day built like dusk from the start. At work in the spa, no appointments booked so she sits at the reception desk alone looking out at the busy slick street, the traffic, listening to cars hiss in passing.

Two men walk by outside the spa's broad windows in soaked white shirts and ties. They look like salespeople or religious fanatics. One tells a joke. She only knows this because the larger guy laughs, then shoves his friend. A thousand shoves between them, but this time the joker trips over the sidewalk where the roots of a tree have heaved up the concrete. The friend stumbles and lurches into the street, wet tires skid, she closes her eyes. An awful sound of metal thumping flesh. A woman cries out, a bird in a fish net. The friend who pushed him wavers, his arms askew, like they might fall off. She thinks she can see them burning in the wet light.

She lurches to the street. Leafless in the rain, she crowds there with other employees from other shops, murmuring in the downpour as the man's friend shudders and leaks blood in the street, limbs at odd angles, a pile of hangers. His blood thins, waters down in the rain runoff, seeps into the storm grate. The sirens. The police. The ambulance. No one talks to the man who pushed him until the police arrive, the man's white shirt clinging to him in the rain, the skin showing through. No one knows what to say to him.

Across the street, two airline stewards, a man and a woman, watch expressionless, each with matching navy blue outfits, rolly suitcases, and umbrellas. A secret council of two, they lean towards one another sharing secret words, attentive audience to the death in the street, the stricken face of the friend who shoved, like they might review the scene later as art. The woman catches sight of Sarah watching them, grabs the man's sleeve and they bolt for the skytrain station, short panicked looks back.

The now friendless man, pale and drowning, turns towards her, the pleading look of a four-year-old, like she might have the answer to all this absurdity and death. She searches her right pocket and pulls out one of her business cards. She can't help him here in the street, can't find words, but maybe later, after the police and the explaining he might need the kind of help she can provide. She hands him the card.

He examines the card. Bows his head slowly, as though he grinds vertebra against vertebra to do it. A tether pulls him back, grips him to his friend, dead in the street. He pockets the card, chin bears down on chest, the rain running down the back of his neck and under his shirt collar.

SARAH HAD THOUGHT about becoming a counselor or a psychiatrist. In the end, she could only afford the year of massage school. Training to be a therapist would have taken seven or eight more years anyway and she chose instead to spend that time helping people. Her high school guidance counselor wrestled with this because he felt the need to provide her with options in their mandatory guidance counselor sessions. He called her stubborn, but she felt fated to this choice. She grew up in a termagant household, gothic in its needs. Her mother with her perpetual torpor and sporadic periods of desperate longing. Her little sister walking into walls and falling down stairs like some desperate, daft heroine. Even their whorish poodle, Phoebe. They all needed her. She didn't mind.

She became the adult in the house the day her father died in a mill accident. They said he dropped his watch into a turbine and, out of reflex, he reached to grab it, was pulled in and every bone in his body smashed, shards cutting into every organ and pureeing him. Just like that. Bad enough to lose a parent, but for him to be beaten to a pulp, mashed into something not resembling himself, well that's another story. How does one grieve for pulp?

A MONTH LATER, less rain, less sleep, only three appointments at the spa but two canceled. Between their magazine flips, Sarah endures Treena in love again.

"He's kinda hairy."

"But you like him?" asks Sarah, trying to scan an article on dogs and massage on the computer.

"What's not to like?"

Treena's answerless answer waits between them. Sarah yawns to change the subject. Kyle bar-hopped out late with the guys last night again and Sarah couldn't sleep with his side of the bed blank. Or at least she told herself this. And then, 3:23 am, his hulking, farting, snuffling, filled that side of the bed, and she lay there puzzling the window and the street light through the blinds and wondered what she'd been waiting for after all.

"He's in a band. I think that's what he said," says Treena, scanning the street outside the window like a magazine with too many ads.

Outside the floor to ceiling glass windows, a large man stands at the curb, his back to them. He doesn't look like he's going to cross. Doesn't look like he's waiting for a ride, or is about to glance up the street for a car approaching. Yet his stillness, expectant, as the pedestrians course on by. He looms alone, waits.

A girl in Sarah's building, the one on the first floor near the elevator, is a puppeteer. One night she showed Sarah the room in her apartment where she builds the puppets. Sarah stood at the threshold, her heart swollen and smothering her lungs. She felt childish, goofy, and a startling plush affection as she held a monkey puppet in her arms, her neighbor cradling a dragon puppet like a wounded forest creature.

And then the woman folded the puppet away into a velvet box, sliding it onto a shelf.

"Why do you put them away?" Sarah asked. "I'd hang them up everywhere. I'd want to always see them."

"Well, they can put a bit of a crimp in your sex life. But, truth be told, when they're not in my hands, I can't bear to look at them. A few motionless seconds and they die."

The man at the curb, inert. Sarah wills him to move.

He turns to the spa window, scans the sign. Tugs open the door, the digital chime sounding. Anxious in his shirt and black tie, he takes a stolid stance in the spa's open, white space.

"Can I help you?" Sarah asks.

The man says nothing, his face a tinge of pink like the tie is preventing the blood from leaving his head.

Treena flops her magazine down on the counter. "You look stressed. Bet you could use a massage. Are you a businessman? Because it looks like you hold your stress in your forehead. That's why so many businessmen go bald. Stress in their brains and forehead wrinkles. They hold their stress there."

The man touches a hand to his temple. Sarah recognizes him then, wants to grab Treena's scattered words in mid-air before they assault this poor man again.

The man reaches out his left hand and places a business card on the counter. Sarah's card.

"Sure, let's get you set up then," says Treena, "Just follow me" she waves and he rounds the counter and shadows after her. Maybe he doesn't speak English. Or maybe he's deaf and just nodding. Sarah feels certain she'd make a terrible deaf person. She would just nod to get by and end up agreeing to terrible things.

She waits five minutes and then knocks as she enters the massage room, finds him face down on the table under the sheet, his pallid broad back hunched there. His body inert, corpse-like, as though the candles in the room are having their light pulled in to him.

"I will be your massage therapist today. Is this your first time?"

He does not answer.

"Is there . . . do you have an injury or something that needs more attention?" Sarah squeezes oil into her hands, rubs them together to warm them. "Okay then, just breathe through this to help your body release the toxins. And let me know if I am applying too much pressure." She reaches out, her hands hovering just over the man's broad back. His body begins to shake. Sarah retreats her hands.

"Sir, are you alright?"

His body continues to shake.

"It's quite common to feel emotional during a massage. The body holds so many things." No response. "Bottles them up."

His shoulders cinch up around his neck, the table shuddering with his inhales, shaking with his weeping exhales. "Just let the feelings flow out of you," she whispers low, aware her voice is tense. His breaths then less drastic, the table stabilizing. "Perhaps some essential oils will help calm you." She drops some lavender in the diffuser in the corner, waves her hands to help the scent waft. She closes her eyes, inhales, exhales, centres herself, but then hears the man cry out, as though sharply jabbed.

She stations herself at the top of the table next to his shoulder and arm, places one hand at the nape of his neck and runs the other down the length of his spine, a grounding gesture, but his back muscles flinch, tense, a fish torqueing on a wooden dock, the sobbing wrings out of him louder.

She steps back, ponders the length of him, her oiled hands, the titles of the books on her bookshelf. Nothing. She sits down in the chair against the wall, his body before her shaking with sobs. She can't just leave him alone. He shouldn't be alone for this. So she sits with her oiled hands face up on her aproned lap, as though making an offering.

His weeping surges, then trickles, then surges, vacillating on. She looks at the clock high on the wall. Only fifteen minutes have passed. Maybe she should ask him questions, help him make meaning from this grief. Maybe later. Expression first.

She considers checking her phone for messages since, face smushed into the headrest, he wouldn't be able to see. Invents instead a game, focusing her attention on his heaving back, wondering if she can witness it just another five minutes. And then another five.

Half an hour past, she thinks to offer him a Kleenex, feels abominable for not offering sooner. Holds back, realizes she wants to give him a Kleenex to make herself feel better, not to help him.

Forty-five minutes into the session, only fifteen left, his body lies still for whole minutes, before his back and shoulders begin to shudder again.

At the end of the hour, Sarah picks up a clean hand towel from the shelf beside her, wipes the oil from her hands and stands, hesitates, measures what volume to use with her voice. "Well, we're out of time today," she calls over his weeping.

The words sound like they belong to a therapist. She's never said them. A massage, until now, was always something that she finished. He must be struck by these words too because the weeping changes to breaths, gasps, even those ebbing. "I'll see you outside when you're ready" she adds, then "Don't worry, there'll be no charge for today," and she slips out of the room.

Sarah leans against the front counter, her palms face up in front of her again. Treena punctuates the quiet with little flips of her magazine pages, licks her finger and then turns another page. Unsanitary, Sarah thinks. Something old women do.

Sarah has a memory, vague in her head, about a neighbor's cat that was attacked by one of the trailer park dogs. How she cared for the cat, washed the blood from its fur, even though it scratched her hands and arms several times. "You know," she says, "You know, my mother once said I have a gift." The cat's owner, a lady in a green rain jacket, came in the morning to take the cat away. She didn't even say thanks.

Treena flips another page, nods. "So how does it work?"

"Well, I'm not sure yet."

"That sounds dangerous," says Treena with an edge of mocking, as she turns back to her magazine, licking her fingers and turning another page.

"Well, sometimes when I am massaging people, I ask them a question in my mind as I put my hands on them."

"My policy is don't ask questions. Makes people think you care."

Across the street two airline stewards with rolly suitcases flank one another, a man and a woman, both with dark hair and serious expressions. They're watching her. No, she thinks, they are thinking of coming in for a manicure and checking out the sign. So familiar.

Treena holds her magazine in front of Sarah's face. *How to make your boyfriend love only you.* "I wonder why people need to feel extraordinary. I mean, look at me. I'm as ordinary as it gets. And I bet I get laid more than a lot of extraordinary folks."

"But wouldn't that make you extraordinary?"

Treena takes the magazine back, perplexed.

Outside the window, the sun shatters off the windshields of passing cars. Just pavement where the stewards had stood.

**SARAH HEELS THE** apartment door closed and locks it, hears the jagged noises of a cartoon show on the upstairs television. Sarah's friend Amy walks dogs for a living and explained to her once how dogs that won't keep eye contact acknowledge your mastery. Last night, Sarah and Andrew managed to make spaghetti, eat in front of the TV watching cartoons, and load the dishwasher without making eye contact. They at last, accidentally, saw each other's reflections in the bathroom mirror while brushing their teeth. Three years, two living together.

Andrew, for her though, cures the chaos. He believes in simplicity, likes the same kind of beer every time, the cheap blue label one, and was baffled by her family when he met them their second Christmas together. "Why are they so loud?" he asked. "They're like those yelling carnies who want you to play the games you can't win." Exactly.

In bed later, he starts that half snore of his. She prefers him asleep, despite the distance vertigo. Sleep turns him gentle. Awake, he bumper cars through the world all elbows, table corners, and unexpected collisions; they can't have peaceful, romantic walks. She rolls over and ponders his bare shoulder above the bedspread. Has she imagined this distance between them? She's imagined such things before. Of course he seems distant; he's asleep with that looming back to her.

Still, she feels it more painfully tonight, contemplates waking him up — even anger would feel better than this melancholy. The pilled sheets against her skin. Damn cheap sheets. She likes his shoulders. Round and muscled. She places her hand on his bare shoulder, the skin cold because he likes to sleep with the window open and his shoulders get cold from the night air slipping in.

He mumbles something she can't understand. She pulls her hand back. Sleepy breaths duvet the room again. She wonders if she imagined that he mumbled. She rests her hand gently on his cold shoulder again, waits for a moment.

He mumbles. Indecipherable.

She takes her hand back. "Honey?" she asks, checking to see if he is awake. She pushes up on her elbows. His sleep has changed. She slides out from under the covers, her toes on the chilled floor, tiptoes around the bed to his side. His face wet, eyes scrunched, shines in the mute light strained through the bedroom blinds. Tears run across his face sideways, dripping onto the pillowcase.

"Honey?" she asks.

"Hrrrrumph" His eyes still clenched closed, oblivious to her.

His tears feel unbearably private, so she pads back to her side of the bed, lies down facing his broad, sleeping back. Then rolls over on her back, pulls the covers up to her throat to keep warm and etch-a-sketches worried thoughts across the blank ceiling, shaking her head to erase them. A gift that makes people cry. What good can come from that?

The next morning, Treena with her flip flip magazines, stews over something that guy of hers did the night before. The front door opens to the same blank faced man, the one who cried. He shuffles up to the counter, chin to chest.

"Good morning," Treena slaps the magazine down on the counter as she pushes up from the chair. Nothing. "Okay, follow me," and she leads him back to the massage room. Sarah sips water from her water bottle, the grey on grey day sliding by outside.

A few minutes later, she knocks, slips into the massage room. As she closes the door, his hands, palms upturned on the massage table seem to burn in the half-light.

"Good morning," she presses the door closed. "Anything coming up or places we should specifically look at?"

Nothing.

She rubs oil on her hands, rubs them together to warm them, and reaches out over his back.

His body begins to tremor, then shake.

She pulls her hands back.

The shaking ceases.

She reaches out, palms hovering over his back again.

Shudder, his shoulders hitch up, chest heaving with sobs.

She moves her hands off, the sobbing ceases.

She rubs them together again, then holds them just an inch off his back. The sobs shaking his rib cage, the table. She closes her eyes. Breathes. Hands held in mercy over the sobbing man's back.

Five hours later, after the man has left, after lunch, after three more clients, none of whom weep, they hit an afternoon lull. Sarah leans against the front counter up against the determined passings of the pedestrians out front, the rush of the traffic. Treena applies first one then another, and then a third perfume sample strip from the magazines sprawled in front of her to the soft insides of her forearms.

"What are you doing?"

"Creating my own scent."

Sarah's forehead clinches. Her throat cinches, breathless.

Maybe she carries something from the morning, from the pale man with the burning hands. She latches on to the emotional states of others, like Velcro. Like adhesive tape, "A Velcro girl," her mother said once. Well, someone did.

"How's that gift you got working out?" mumbles Treena, rubbing another scent across the inside of her wrist.

"What?"

"Your gift?" Treena says a little louder, like she's talking to an idiot.

"Oh. Think I spoke too soon."

"Maybe it's a subtle gift."

Sarah sneezes, the perfume cloud that is Treena overwhelming her. "Kinda like your perfume."

"Well, might be for the best. Gifts never come free."

Treena says so little that makes sense that this outburst seems like an omen. The traffic thickens, clutters the air outside the glass aquarium walls of the spa.

Sarah locks up, wanders home, but then halfway there, at the outdoor concrete pond shaped like a leaf, wonders if she wants to stray further.

At home, she drifts between the rooms, finds Andrew in the bedroom passed out, remote control in his hand, the bedroom TV chattering sitcom laughter. A half-eaten pizza in the box on the bedside table presents itself like a symptom. Andrew eats pizza when depressed. This worries her. His mouth sags open, one small line of drool forming, tomato sauce in the corner of his mouth.

She nukes a diet frozen lasagna, her own symptom, then eats it leaning against the kitchen counter. After, she shuffles up the stairs, brushes her teeth, her tongue, foregoes flossing. Andrew has slid under the covers, trying out his light snore, the TV nattering some infomercial. She sits down on her side of the bed, glazed-eyed in front of the TV and the helpful people wondering how they ever lived without the Abdominal Crunch Master 2000.

Andrew snorts and rolls over towards his side of the bed. She doesn't know what her hands can do. She only knows that Andrew cried. When his mother called to say that they had had to put down Scout, the family American spaniel, he had sat on the couch and stared at The Shopping Network channel for a full hour, the control in his hand, the only emotion a slight squint to his eyes as though he was parapsychically attempting to light fire to the presenters and their budgie banter. Now, based on his scrunched up face and the deluge of tears, much worse things could happen if he held this in.

When they first started dating, she felt such relief at the way he put emotions away into boxes and closets, tidy. The complete opposite of her histrionic soap opera family. But his system lacked a logic and all emotions went into one junk drawer that tortured itself into an undifferentiated elasticyarntwisttieketchuppack mess. She has developed a way of getting him to talk: she warns him days in advance if they need to discuss something and then has to pretend she doesn't see him growling and kicking at the leg trap. She's tired of coordinating any form of communication between them. And all this containment must wear on him, a slow cancerous erosion. If her hands can release these emotions, then she could be helping him.

She rubs her hands together then holds them over his back, squeezing her eyes closed, sending every bit of energy she can through them to him.

He mutters.

She pulls her hands back. She rounds to his side of the bed, kneels down, rubs her hands together again, and holds them over his shoulder. She sees tears well in the corners of his eyes; she leans in, her ear close to his mouth and feels his breath on her ear. That mouth of his, kissable, even with the drool. She decides to try again, hovers, ear near his mouth, hands over his shoulder, concentrates.

He mutters. It sounds like "fortune cookie." Or "Don't stand near me." Tears run down his sideways face, across the bridge of his nose, down his cheek and soak the pillow.

She leans back, cross-legged on the floor, wants to wipe his tears, but knows she would wake him then. So she holds her hands in her lap in front of her, turning his mutterings over in her head like hard candy in her mouth. He snorts, rolls over on his back.

She crosses back to her side of the bed, lies back down. Is she breaking him?

Ragged and torn sleep.

Alarm, shower, clothes, toast, bus, bitter coffee from the Greek place on the corner.

At work, she unlocks the door, flips the light switches, presses the power button on the stereo, the spa insistently and energetically tranquil despite her suffering thoughts. She languishes at the counter, convinced she already broke him.

"I think I've found my gift," says Treena, chewing the last life out of a piece of gum. Gum before noon seems weird to Sarah. "Turns out I am really good with dogs. And children."

Morning traffic a plethora of colourless colours — black, silver, silver, champagne, black, white — pulsing by the other side of the glass.

"But you hate dogs. And children."

Treena shrugs. "Like I said. Every gift has a downside."

The front door opens and the weeping man walks in. Less asphalt coloured than usual, a little boy smile springs up the corners of his mouth.

"You can go right in," Treena tells him. "Sarah will be in in a moment."

The man pads down the hall to the massage room and closes the door.

"You must have a gift," whispers Treena, eyes wide like she's reading a children's story. "That's the guy's first smile ever. Bet since birth. We should notify his mother. It's a miracle."

Sarah remembers his smile on the street with his friend, the moment before the shove. "Be nice."

"Those jeans are awful, but he looks like he has a cute ass. Does he?"

Sarah lurches up, a tilting smile, frictions her hands together. "Patient confidentiality."

"That applies to massage?"

"It does now."

Despite the smile, he returns every day for the next week. Though she never touches him, he still sobs a small symphony each session.

Nights, she lies in bed listening to Andrew's sobs, his growing misery, a shadow crushing its weight on her ribcage. Still, each night she crosses to his side of the bed, can't stop herself from laying hands on him. Like the old lady who swallowed a fly, once you swallow the spider you just have to keep going. Whatever this gift is, Sarah fears it's limited to making grown men cry.

Then, a week after the blank man's first smile, she closes the door for their regular session, rubs her hands together, pauses this time, the room feeling different, a hue more light. She hovers her hands over the man's back.

Nothing. No weeping. No shaking. Just the heat radiating from his skin.

She reaches behind her to the shelf, adds oil to her hands and rubs them together more vigorously. Closing her eyes and, scrunching them together, she tries to send all the energy she can through her hands as she places them over the man's back.

Nothing. No tremor. No sobbing.

After a moment, the man dogs up on his elbows, twists his face towards her. "Everything okay?"

"What?" she says, alarmed to hear his voice.

The pain, the grief that sallowed his face have eased.

"I was waiting for you to ask me that question you ask."

"Question?"

"If there is anything particular we need to focus on this week or something like that."

"Oh. That," she massages her hands together.

"Yeah"

"Okay. Anything in particular you want to work on this week?"

"No. Just the usual," he says, the same little boy smile springing up. He untwists and settles back on the massage table. Sarah places one hand at the top of his neck, runs the other down the length of his spine and rests it there at the base of his spine. No shaking, no weeping, just the slow rise then exhale of his back on the table.

After a full massage, no weeping at all, Sarah sits at the front desk, her hands on the counter in front of her. She guesses it's progress. The man didn't cry today. Or she's lost her gift. The door to the massage room opens and the man exits, shirt collar loose and tie hanging from his hand. At the counter, he hands over his credit card.

"Drink lots of water," Sarah feels odd, finally able to use the script she uses post actual massage.

The man nods, an open-collared smile. "Thanks."

"Have a nice day," Sarah adds, passing him his receipt.

He stops on the sidewalk outside, back to her, holds his face up to the sun.

Treena, coming back from lunch, walks up to the man, touches him on the shoulder, draws his attention from the sun to her, touches him on the bicep to laugh at something she says.

Treena flirts with the subtlety of a piranha. The man says something back, chuckling.

Treena yanks open the door to the spa and saunters up to the counter "Five, four, three —"

"What are you doing?"

"Did my own reconnaissance. He has a nice butt."

"I mean the countdown."

"Oh," she waves over her shoulder towards the man then, leans in conspiratorially as though the man might hear from outside. "I count so that he has time to check me out and miss me."

Sarah leans back, eyes winced against Treena's *Cosmopolitan* machinations.

"It's a four-part system: touch him on a safe body part, give eye contact, take it all away, then make him wait and remind him of the sexy goodness."

"I thought we weren't supposed to date clients."

"But he's not. Not mine anyway. He says you cured him. That's some gift you got."

"I don't understand."

"What's not to understand? You saw that smile."

Sarah squints out at the sunny street, pedestrians walking a burnished parade in the afternoon sun. Even the traffic flowing, not rushing, no honks. She decides to try once more. If she helped this man, maybe she can help Andrew.

After work she swims laps at the Aquatics Centre down by the beach, imagining some cleansing ritual as she thrashes through the water, then focuses on a rhythm, preparing.

The wall clock reads 7:36 pm as she drops her keys on the hall shelf, perplexed to find the apartment entirely dark except the low gloom of the streetlights through the living room window. Andrew must have gone out. Flipping on lights as she wrestles her shoes off, TV chatters echo from the bedroom.

Andrew curled up, hugging a pillow, the TV mumbling at him from across the room, and an empty bowl of ice cream on the nightstand. He'd left her a message earlier. He'd called in sick to work, just felt off, dizzy, glum.

She feels a bit like she's reading his diary, but like she's reading a diary he's written in some language she does not know. No justifying it, she knows she betrays him by doing this if only because she can't imagine telling him: "When you go to sleep at night, I place my hands on you, looking for you to tell me your secrets."

Yes, she wants to know his secrets. This man, the one she knows mostly via voicemails and the sounds of his snores and late night crying now, has gone some place she can't follow. She searches for some sign of what he can't tell her, a sign so she can anticipate the wreckage before she is waist-deep. An early warning to protect her from this sadness that wells up and out of him and what it heralds.

In the bathroom, a staring contest with her conscience in the mirror, she dollops cold cream on the backs of both hands and rubs the cream up to her elbows and back.

She perches on her side of the bed where the blankets are still tucked in, stalling, willing herself to just shut out the light, lie down to sleep. But she knows she won't. Back to standing on the cold floor.

His sleeping face, that slack bottom lip, another line of drool slowly forming from his mouth to the pillow as he snuffle-sleeps on his stomach. She rubs her hands together, closes her eyes, willing her hands to comfort him, ease him to utter what he won't say. She reaches her hands over him, hovering an inch from that wide, broad back she loves, and she stares into his sleepy face, ready.

He mutters, legs scissor jerk, and she holds her breath, prepared to bolt back to her side of the bed if he wakes, but holds her hands steady. This must work. She doesn't want to pry anymore.

She burns her concentration into her hands, willing this apparent gift to rupture the space between them.

His chest trembles, shudders, and then the sobs crack out of him. A torrent of tears glisten his face. The sobs.

She realizes, now with the sobs, that she has only ever seen him cry in his sleep, and certainly has never heard him sob. Awake, he lives his moments as happy as a golden retriever, one of the older more chill ones. And now, where does he find this root of sorrow?

She thinks of how the man from the spa no longer cries, how his grief abated. In this slippage she recognizes her gift, how she removed his grief in small handfuls and carried it home to Andrew, so now Andrew wrestles with a grief not his own. She flees to the bathroom, pumps gobs of soap from the dispenser, digs around under the sink and finds the scrub brush, then scrubs her hands, scrubs them until they're torn and red. Rinses them under scalding water. Silly. Making her skin raw can't cleanse her of the troubles she's carried from one man to the other. Indeed, she herself carries nothing, remains immune to the harm she ferried. Her distressed red hands ragged, a different grief cinches around her, crushes her ribs against one another, crumples her to the floor against the tub.

Despite this burden of sadness she carried to him, Andrew sleeps. Maybe the grief menaces him less because it belongs to the man with the shirt and tie. She reaches for the cold cream, dollops more on her hands, and slowly, ever so slowly, smooths it over the rawness. She remembers the man from the spa, his new smile, how he chuckled and flirted back with Treena. What if Sarah carried something Golden Retriever from Andrew back to that man?

At breakfast, Andrew eats his cereal with the ardor of a tree sloth. "He doesn't love me anymore," she thinks. She can guess he will call into work sick again today. She suggests they both take the day off and go to the beach, or a movie, that latest Schwarzenegger. Andrew paddles the cereal around in the milk with his spoon, shakes his head, "Work." Sarah leaves the apartment before him, the guilt knitting itself down her spine.

A fully booked morning, then a brief break for lunch where mid-salad she watches Treena and the blank man off in search of lunch. She helms the front counter by herself, her hands in her lap, pondering this backwards gift. Outside in the sun, the traffic seems lighter, just masses of colour and air. On the other side of the street, two airline stewards, rolly suitcases, watch her.

Sarah leaves the safety of the front counter, steps out into the street.

Caught, they bolt down the street to the corner, running, the rolly suitcases bouncing on their tiny wheels behind them, but at the corner, they choose converging directions and collide, crashing to the street corner in a tangle of suitcases and limbs. They have taken a man down with them, a narrow parenthetical man, rib cage slim to nothing. One of the stewards staggers up from the ground, rubbing her strained neck. She pulls the other up. They both glance across the street at Sarah then rush off, leaving the lean man still on the concrete, examining his scuffed palms, trying to get his feet back under him. He staggers up, chuckles, blushing away the collision, looks up at a piece of the blue sky beaming through the towers. Sarah waves, crosses the street to him to help. A happy man like that could endure more than his share of grief. He'll hardly notice a little sadness.

SINAI

*"One by one, they were all becoming shades.*
*Better pass boldly into that other world,*
*in the full glory of some passion, than fade*
*and wither dismally with age."*

— "THE DEAD," JAMES JOYCE

# SINAI

**THE TAXI STUTTERS**, coughs, then with a lurch runs off the road
and stalls. Eric looks across at the other two travellers for concern
on their faces, but the American girl, sitting against the other
door, looks more angry, and the Swede is asleep between them,
slack jawed and head resting on her. Either sweat or drool has left
a stain on the girl's shoulder. The American girl says something
to the taxi driver in French. Eric didn't expect that his high school
French was going to be called into use, but several of the locals
spoke it more fluently than English thanks to Napoleon and his
desire to occupy Egypt. Worse, this angry girl from Connecticut
speaks it almost fluently, and he, a Canadian, barely knows how
to say hello. He thinks he can detect a furrow of worry between
her eyebrows and in the rapid pace of her questions to the taxi
driver. Through the windshield, the late afternoon sun is beat-
ing them to Cairo. Stalled at the roadside, the air in the cab is
swallowing itself in the still heat. Judging by her tone they aren't
going anywhere soon so Eric opens the cab door, steps out into
the dirt and rubble by the roadside. They passed a decaying tank
a few miles back. He wonders if there might be anything more to
see. The American girl's tone is getting louder, the words rushing
out of her.

He's not used to this landscape, not used to hills and mountains without trees, a martian terrain of burnt orange rocks and
dirt held down by thrumming blue sky. He has to piss. He decides
to climb the small bluff next to the road, take a leak on the other
side and see what else is around.

Yards from cresting the top, his feet slip on the rock strewn side of the bluff and he falls on his hands, palms burning on the gravel. He hesitates on all fours on the dirt incline to steady himself. He steps one foot towards his hands and carefully rises, the desert staining his palms and pant legs, the kind of dirty dirt that gets into everything, sticks to his fingers even when he tries to brush it off. The American girl and the taxi driver have gotten out of the cab. They don't look up at him, could care less about the cascading noise of the rocks sliding down the slope from where he stumbled.

He scrambles more quickly, lower to the ground, grabbing purchase on the stones and then crests the hill.

From there, a sea of other hills like waves of rock stretch out indifferent under the melancholy sky hanging far above. Behind him, the thin scar of a road winds, endless, in both directions wandering off to meet itself on some other continent.

Maybe a mile away he can see another bluff. He thinks he sees, yes, a red cloth billowing in the wind, sudden — why didn't he see it before? Maybe someone lives there. Back down at the cab, through the back window, the Swede's lopsided sleeping head. The cab driver has opened the hood of the car and stands back, regarding its workings with some suspicion. The American girl pushes him out of the way and leans under the hood. Eric's convinced he can see the cab driver's confused look from the top of the bluff. Eric wouldn't be surprised if this girl and her peculiar collection of skills might be able to fix the cab.

Another cab bears down on them from the east. Cabs seem to be the preferred mode of transportation on the Sinai. Three travellers can pay less than bus fare and they won't be jammed up against chain smokers and insidious hands the way they would on the buses. He barely knows these two other travellers, the narcoleptic Swede and the angry American, but they had all lounged in Dahab's cafés and open restaurants, eaten the massive plates of beans and rice, and gnarled chicken legs, knocked away the flies, knocked them away again for too many days. The flies won in the end. Eric now ate whole meals with the flies ecstatically camping around his mouth and hands, too weary to swat them away in the heat.

After two weeks in that village, Eric began to wonder if he would ever leave. He'd found a copy of *The Odyssey* in the little café. He read it in the café in the morning until it got too hot, then he napped the afternoon away in the small huts that rented for the price of a cup of coffee back home, nothing but a grey, dusty stained mattress on the dirt floor, a single light bulb he left off to avoid the bleak detritus. Days spent slipping in and out of sleep in that earthen tomb, sometimes reading the book if he could see the words in the light leaking under the door, stumbling out to one of the Bedouin cafés along the water for a meal, to succumb to the flies once a day. One afternoon, after maybe his second nap, he read the section where Ulysses's men meet the Lotus Eaters. He realized he hadn't been homesick in a while. Hadn't talked to his mother in weeks. A sudden lurch under his ribs, toe reaching for the sea floor and finding it's fallen away. He knew he had to pack up and leave this place. Or never leave.

The red swath on the bluff batters in the wind, and he wonders how far? Could he hasten there and back before they finish repairing the cab? Down below, the baffled cab driver suffers the angry American girl. The other cab that pulled over now pulls away and diminishes towards Cairo, its passengers fishbowling through the rear window, glad their cab's not broken down in the middle of the Sinai.

He scrambles down the last rocks on the far side of the hill and reaches the desert floor. He realizes then this is a real desert and so might be full of real snakes and scorpions, willing his eyes to scour the rocks and pebbles he walks on while not losing sight of the red tear. Dahab squats between a low ridge of mountains and the red sea so they had to worry more about stepping on sea urchins and the maddening effects of molesting flies than the dangers of desert critters like scorpions.

He looks back toward the road, but the bluff obscures the cab and the travellers. They won't leave without him. Well, the Swede wouldn't but he's asleep. Eric's come this far though. He wants to see what that swath of cloth is. Maybe a base left over from the war with Israel. Maybe a Bedouin hut, an actual Bedouin though and not the ones he found in Dahab. The American girl's French would come in handy. Discernible now, the cloth is an arterial red, maybe scarlet once, but filthed by the sand.

Behind him now, the road is far off. A breeze from the north — taste of salt, held to the cool cheek of the sea — washes the day off. He's free from the taxi, the other travellers, the cab's wrangy gum wrapper, cigarette butt, and discarded water bottle jetsam of all the travellers before him. He must be halfway to the red tumult of fabric now, and the sun seems to have slipped and fallen halfway to the horizon. He should turn back. But just then he's convinced he can hear a slap of the dried blood red banner snapping against itself in the wind. He hears the snap again. A sign. He breaks into a clunking hiking boot jog.

The flag is not a flag at all. He stops in his tracks, face white, as the woman turns, wraps the billowing venous red cloth around her shoulder once and then again, drawing in the slack, then ascends the ridge and falls away from him. She must have stood there, still as a caryatid in the desert, for half an hour. She must have seen him. So why did she quit him now? And what could she be doing out here in the desert?

He finds the base of the bluff, rushes to climb the side, trying to draw together his rudimentary French so he can remember how to say hello in case she doesn't speak English. *Qu'est-ce que vous faites ici?* But what are the chances he will understand her reply.

He crests the bluff. No shelter, no tent, nor any sign of the woman. The road and the taxi, far off now, the sun, hunkering down to the horizon.

Then, in the East, a slash of red again, like she's unwound the clot of cloth into the wind, the gusts stronger now as the sun goes down. Somehow she's raced on ahead, crests the next bluff in the distance. He can make it back to the cab if he jogs, if he doesn't stop to catch his breath. He wonders what will happen to his luggage if the American and the Swede drive on without him. He'll search them out in Cairo. They'll hold the backpack for him — the decent thing to do. The sun falls faster. She stands clot red on the next bluff, a taunt. He stands halfway between the road and her, caught between two stories. Really only one.


AT FIRST, it took me months to recognize her, to distinguish her from the sand storms, the scuttling of blue necked lizards, and the kettling of the vultures waiting for a wake. Her orbit and wandering at first just seemed part of the days, the way a fly in a window sounds like summer. Slowly she came into focus, her hands first. For I remember her hands, from when we knew each other as children. Well, not children, but we were young. Her hands a weary Ghawazi dancer's at the end of a staggering night. I met a Ghawazi dancer once. She came with other wanderers, the lurid and itchy souls who made pilgrimage here in the decades after I was brought back from the dead, with their misconceptions, their shallow faith that I might have answers.

I didn't. I don't.

I could almost smile at the thought, but that would take weeks.

Blue-green veins weave their way over the bones of what those hands once were, but she holds them the same, straight at her sides, palms slightly forward as though she is listening quietly with them, always waiting to begin.

She wasn't beautiful. Eyes dark like mashed dates, immodest pulpy mouth, and a long lash of a neck, like she had been carried around by the scruff as a child. Nothing remarkable. But it was her defiance, how she met each stranger with a full stare and the slightest mocking curve to her mouth. Men did not come to her for nurture, comfort, a jug of goat's milk and bread on her bedside table. She did not lie back for a man, but met him chest to chest. Men, he imagined, were drawn to her because they were unsure they could win. And that uncertainty was more thrilling than the certainties of the other women in the huts on the east side of the city walls. Defiance gave her the smartness of a blade or a weapon. Now what slid through the desert was a shadow.

I remember her. I know I should remember her. I want to. Memories of her are held like water in sand, and I recall moments. Her on a bridge, a glass scarab she pocketed from a vendor she'd tricked into looking at her lips. Her in a dark room, with him, one afternoon when I went looking for him. Him. *Hibibi,* she whispers, the shadows of an afternoon nap sticking to them like honey.

I should remember her the way he would, not how I would with my lime gaze. I remember her waist, the way a man's hands might hold it in the circumference of his hands, how her bottom lip rested arrogant, twice as thick as her thin top lip. She refused to swim with us at the river bed south of town, she told me in confidence once, because when her hair got wet it would no longer hide her ears, how they stood out from her head like handles on a jug. Her perfume, then, Cyprinum from Egypt, probably brought by a merchant seeking to be a favourite of hers, a man who knew not to cloud her in florals: henna, cardamom, cinnamon, myrrh and southernwood – nothing sweet about her.

Her hair is blacker now. She must dye it. I suspect she has the same ears. She definitely has the same long forehead and she has found some way to keep her lips plump, though there is an appearance of effort, slight disfigurement, even a scar in the corner of her mouth. She has about her now an air of carpentry and craft.

Not water, memory is an Ariadne thread and each memory tugs with it another. She meant for this to be the case as she circles out there in the desert, waiting for my memory to unravel. Tug. She turns away from me now, those rags she's worn for all these histories snapping in the wind.

Her question coming, a dark creature under the sand, but I licked dry all my waiting long ago. A delirium of days passes over my face like flies. Yes, the flies. I am fly-blown and carcass, parchment texture of wasp's nest. She circles. Waiting like a fresh cut. A decrepit, moth-eaten woman pretending she can still be coy. I don't understand. I am closing my eyes. It may take some time, these crusted lids losing to the sunset and sinking light.

**HE'S WAITED TOO LONG.** The sun limns the horizon, he cannot make it back to the taxi before dark. He has to follow her. He climbs down the other side of the bluff, sets off at a light jog, watching the ground. He's pretty sure, now that he thinks about it, that scorpions come out at night. Maybe he can catch up to her before the last shard of sun goes. But what if she disappears again, appears on another bluff further still? What then. What he feels isn't fear exactly. He remembers his book back in the cab. He is off the map, face to the edge of whatever might come next.

She waits on the bluff, her robes like blood spreading across a streambed. *Qu'est-ce que tu fais ici?* He practices in his head. How to hear the answer. He slows to a walk to catch his breath. The sand gathering between his toes, around his heels in the boots. His eyes are tired, grainy. Maybe he can find a rock on the next bluff where he can wedge himself, break from the wind, sleep in a bed of sand.

Closer, her details articulate. Her head wrapped in a lighter red fabric, covered from the sun, the wind, maybe god. He imagines he will part the robes protecting her face, how she will be older than him but a noble beauty, mouth still full, small stiches of age in the corners, faint creases of time fanning out from her eyes. Her eyes ambered, she could say anything and these eyes would still reassure you that all is love. Exquisite. She will be older than him, a woman who has known men, but that was decades ago. He understands longing. He hasn't known women for a while. He thought about kissing the American girl's complaint of a mouth, but decided against it. She would have corrected his technique, certainly. Besides, the Swede in his pale pretty giraffe way had lurched into her lap and ended that possibility. This woman though, her mouth would be round but languishing at the edges. Cinnamon with melancholy. Thirsty.

And then she turns, draws the billowing robe into her, wraps it around her shoulders again, retreats from him, down the other side of the bluff. The sun lets go and falls off the edge.

He draws his cold arms out of the sleeves of the shirt and folds them under it, across his bare chest, conserving heat. He starts to jog again, thinking this might keep him warm. If she has raced on ahead, how far can she have gone now.

He slows his pace, this bluff steeper, the rocks cascading down behind him. He clenches his arms tighter to his chest, shivering.

Then halfway up the larger stones give way to gravel and his foot slips and, armless, he falls forward, his right shoulder and forehead sliding into the gravel. Stupid. He lies there, forehead and shoulder burning raw from where they hit the gravel, and yet relieved not to be walking or running. Gives into the ground, the most certain thing he's felt. The pain a close second. His eyes water.

She's getting away. He rolls onto his back, pushes his arms back through his sleeves, then reaches up to his temple where he can feel a stinging wetness. He touches his fingers to the wetness tentatively, breath tangled in his ribs, then holds his hand in front of his face. Blood. Not much. Thickening already. He touches the blood to his tongue, tastes it metal and salty. The sky above him darkens, the blue seeping away to the west. Cold now. The stinging, the blood on his tongue, the sky swallowing the light, he almost forgets himself, forgets what he was questing for. Then he recalls, and struggles to his hands, then feet, the rock face rising up above him, whispering for him to climb.

He climbs the rest of the way up the side of the bluff, crests. This bluff is larger, broad across the top. He pauses. Nothing but desert and other bluffs as far as he can see in any direction. No lanterns flicker on to replace the fading light. No fires. Just the thin remains of the sunset at the horizon now, a pale light lamenting, and a few stars uncertain. He feels the shift. Ever since the cab drove away from the Lotus Eater days of Dahab, he had been thinking he was on his way home now. In that moment, the desert an expanding drowning carelessness around him, he can no longer remember a home. At the same time the most peculiar loneliness spreads chill like rubbing alcohol across his skin. At the edge looking out at the dark, the air thinning and bare to the cold blue sky, lost at last.

**SHE'S NOT ALONE**. Trailing after her, a small figure, this man with the odd clothes, the bright blue top. Does he follow or does she lead? Always so confusing with her. From here I can see him clearly enough. Something familiar. His neck drawn uncommonly long, a little noble, a little vulnerable to French guillotines and women with corrupt mouths. I remember a neck like this, the nape of neck stretching up, as though at the top of that neck one might see better, gather a better perspective.

This man of hers turns, and green eyes. Green eyes. I remember. I know why she's come, why after these thousands of years. How many life spans. Not clearly, just that I know why she's come specifically, that she plagues me about him, the one we both knew. What she would have me remember is what I wanted to forget most. Longing.

She vultures in a wide arc now. She has a plaything. After all these thousands of years how she can still be amused by men still surprises me. A faded image, yet I prefer her now, age wresting a trace of vulnerability in the lines of her corners. But gut the broiling dog corpse and beneath the fur the maggots swarm and dervish. I knew she'd be back.

Curiosity died with me. He brought this body back, but not all of me returned with it. What remains: a slim numbness to the beauty of leaves on the olive trees, an insensitivity to stars, even the thick dusted night sky out here in the desert, a lack of compassion for the Bedouin children with skinned knees and dirt in their eyes. Yet I remember that I used to feel these things, feel and taste and lose breath and even weep. Now just memories. Lost when I died, or did longing just swallow the other emotions, diminish me to this corpse, this husk.

They will name their lepers after me. If it was love that compelled him to bring me back, there was little hope that love would live on. He didn't have much time left. He sat with me one night, after he brought me back. Sat and I looked out over the yard, while he looked up at the sky gaudy above us. I could hear him shift in the chair, feel him struggle not to speak, not to look at me. After it was as before, me wanting him with a hankering like a bird in a fist. Only now there was no chance he would lie with me by the river, the sounds of the water on rocks, the stars upstaging the fecund, mineral algae scent of the river's breath, his cheek on the corner of my rib cage tilted up. Desire swallowed me up, time had its way, leaving this heart a pebble in a paper wasp hive. A cage full of whispers and dry breath.

I am not anaesthesia. I am only made for this interminable, salt flat longing. Waiting warps time. Stretches it until the flesh almost gives way. Yet, wondering slivered under the fingernails. Why she is back now, with some new pet? She should leave me be.


THE NEXT STEP IS the void. The stars show only the suggestion of the ground. He decides to fall back on that rule his mother had for when he was lost in a department store: stay right where you are. Though it would help if he could sit down on the linoleum of the department store, under the clothes racks, and see all the various legs of the women shoppers, the nylons, the short, medium, and long skirts, the heels, the woman who cut herself shaving her legs, the woman whose veins run too close to the surface. From there he might be able to identify his mother's thin ankles, the perennial flats she wore in primary colours, might be able to find her in the retail underbrush. But in the Sinai, only the sand, the stone, the sky and him. He finds a waist-high stone on the bluff, and huddles down on the leeway side of it, in the shadow of the wind, backs himself as close to the stone as he can and huddles into a ball for warmth. A little sleep. A little rest. She has to sleep too, probably shelters nearby.

The American and the Swede have certainly departed without him. He can probably track them down in Cairo. Hopefully they hold on to his luggage and don't just abandon it. She's cruel, the American, but not in that way. He'd tried to kiss her a couple of nights ago. At the bar, the three of them and a couple of Australians had been lounging around the low table ravaged by flies, sipping awful, watery beer. The Swede was telling the Aussies a story Eric had already heard him tell four times to travellers of three different nationalities. He took a gulp of the beer to swallow down the odd edge of anger, half boredom, half claustrophobia under the weight of the Swede's meandering, verbless stories. He sat up, like he might go somewhere, anywhere but this fly-blown strip of sand looking out over the red mountains and sea. She sat up in that moment too so they were suddenly sitting beside each other. He leaned in to kiss her, her slightly drunk mouth hanging unawares. She blurted a laugh before his lips could connect, covered her mouth.

"I thought —"

"I was getting up to pee," she said shaking her head. She lurched up and stumbled from the room laughing to herself. Cruel.

He had had the notion that in other countries he'd be able to kiss girls more easily. That he would, as a traveller, be more bold. Imagining it made it a little so. He had kissed four women in the last four months of travelling. He decided that the American girl was probably a terrible kisser, what with the anger and the sullen mouth and all. Then when she came back from the bathroom she laid down next to the Swede and started making out with him. Eric gulped another mouthful of his beer, warm now, thankful at least that she had silenced the Swede's damn story.

Eric imagines them warm in the throng of Cairo now, the two of them. Out here in the desert, abandoned by the sun he shivers as the sky chases the last light. A void salted with stars, frigid and ancient looms over him. He doesn't sleep so much as his thoughts go numb. He loses time. Centuries seem to pass, agony, as he waits for the sun to rise again, naked and pale, weary from its journey to the other side.

**AFTER HE BROUGHT ME** back to life, my sister Mary claimed it was because she asked. Neither of my sisters knew what he and I meant to one another. Then my other sister, Martha, argued the same. She had asked. He had obliged. Though in the end, regardless, they both followed me here, cared for me, to placate my mother and be away from her grief.

Years after they both left and word came back of their deaths, there would be others who would come. It seemed the Marys of the world are drawn here. First, of course, my sister, confused and looking for explanation. Then after a time, other Marys. Mair, Maire, Mal, Mame, Mamie, Manette, Mare, Maree, Maridel, Marlo, Masha, Moll . . . Written in the sand, erased, then written again. Small hands, withered hands, smooth, angular like utensils, round like bread loafs. They wash my feet, then wash them again. They bring thick crusted bread, like stones, earthen bowls of olives, greens and blacks, pickles, jugs of wine, and we watch it all decay, collapse under the fury of the flies. Remove the dishes and then sacrifice more. Their questions dirtied the air like blue bottle flies. I only offered these travellers the space at my feet for food to rot. Seems like an odd joke, though, the repetition of their name. And they each came knowing something of my story. Waited like more of it would be revealed, though I gave up words long ago.

The last Mary was Italian. Maybe Spanish. She hardly ever spoke, though once she asked a question, "How long?" and I decided it was an apt name for this place. More places should be named questions. And, of course, she who staggers out there on the sand, pretending coy but really forlorn, she is also a Mary.

The Mary before the first Mary. She exceeds all the rest, even my sister, as though she carries in her corrupt head of hair one strand for each of them, one strand for each of their longings.

That Mary, out there, brandishes all these other desires like badges. I wear them like mottled sores. She floats over the sand, skin drinking up each errant desire, the travellers, the Marys, lost Bedouins, a magpie for others' hankerings. She is ellipses too, like me, an open-ended story, bleeding.

**A PALING**, the thinnest film of sky returning. No roosters, no other signs other than the coming of the light. Eric's muscles ache from shivering, his jaw from clenching in the cold. He leans forward, freeing his hands to push him to his feet, staggers like he is born again or dying. The sand is in everything, his mouth, his shoes, the grit in every rut of his fingerprint. He staggers to the edge of the bluff where he last saw her disappear. He expects to see her on the next bluff in the distance, but she is not there. Is this it? End of the story. But he doesn't want to go back now. He's down to nothing but one foot in front of the next. If he walks long enough in one direction, maybe this one, he has to reach water. The red sea flanks the Sinai on two sides and the Mediterranean the other side. He can't stay lost. Can he.

The next bluff pinks with the first rays of the sunrise, a jagged sleeping form waiting. He can't stop shivering. Random, staggering images come into his mind. The American girl, her ratty boy-red baseball cap, the Swede with his drowsy, slack jaw, probably still sleeping. Even his mother, across the sea, the ocean, and a continent from him now. He knows she sleeps with one of his old t-shirts. Like this will keep him safe. She knew he would leave. Last Valentine's, a few months before he left, she sent him framed baby photos of himself. He couldn't bring himself to hang them, these pictures weighed down by her mother love. He pictures her in amongst her beer steins and her silk paintings, her friends always dropping by. She must miss him. What will she think of this, his death? Will she wonder why he wandered off into the desert? This might be what she feared.

He's walking the way that always used to make his brother laugh, his arms moving twice as fast as his legs, a wheat thresher or a swamp hovercraft.

"Do you think they make you go faster?" he asked once.

"I dunno. Try it."

And his brother had set off flailing, looking down as he walked through his swinging arms. Like watching the world through the flares of a strobe light, his brother noted. They both tried it then, swinging their arms and pacing the grass in front of the house. Their mother had called from the kitchen window to stop, that they were scaring the neighbours.

He might not be going faster, but his arms aren't numb with the cold anymore. Far to his right, something moving across the desert. The tumult of her robes, a red jellyfish in torrid currents, upended and ravaged. No wind where he stands, the morning breathless, so he can't imagine what wind storm would be required to hurtle those contorted robes across the sand that way. He hesitates, watching the sun rise reluctantly, like it might set again, in what must be the east.

SHE DISCARDS THIS blue-clad lost boy. Races off so now he is alone, awry with fear, his head jerking to see the source of each noise around him. He walks too upright, stilted, awkward like he doesn't know where to put his hands, not like the boys from the medina with their leanings and their languishes and hand in hand love.

Why did she bring him here? That long neck, that sharp chin and rounded jaw, a man of contrasts. She brought him here to torment me, it's certain, but why?

This, just the sort of game she is made for, her stern flanks, her hunger persisting, her lost laugh among the olive branches. No, she's not about usefulness or scripture or comfort. She is the worst of her kind.

Something about a thirsty man. *Soif,* the French say. Sounds more like the word should. Salt on length of cocked neck, breath furtive, irony and earthy. I inhale, falter. When did I lose my ability to smell?

What was the last smell? Was it before he raised me, brought me back? No, much later. So little to smell here, the sand, the decay of food left by travellers at my feet, so my senses reached out across the desert, distant scents delivered like letters thanks to the winds. Grit flung heat of Khamaseen from the south, Sirocco and its maladies in fever dreams, short bursts of the Simoom from the south and east, like bone dry hands suffocating my face, gasping your lungs to dry river beds. I knew a Simoom once that left cattle, camels, birds suffocated and scorched on their feet; fruit trees all along the river dropped their fruit like burnt dresses, jugs of water left on café tables cracked open, their water evaporating then gone, and a man caught in a felucca on the river was blistered red, blinded, saved only once he flung himself in the river.

These troubling winds are my companions now. All harsh but they carry swatches of other lives under their breaths: the green relief of gardens and vines inhaling after a July rain on a cliff-edged island in the sea north of here. The dusty neck of a thin, cinnamon stick of a man building a mud abode south past the roots of the Nile. The spilt milk and pee smell of a boy in Tripoli, brushing a fuzzy leaf of mint across his round cheek. How many hundreds of years ago did it cease, did the scents of all these begin blowing past me? My companions have all fallen silent.

He stands so close to me now, oblivious, his limbs in relief and soft focus, his patchy beard scruff, the soft smooth spot behind his ear, the supple muscles along his arms, the vee of his back. And no scent. A map of scents I once knew, now scentless. Almost. He's almost him. The differences between them blur, as though I am bent on bringing him back from the dead.

If I cannot smell, though, how will I remember?

I remember the first time I saw her. A woman was refusing to sell her lentils at the market, her eyes pinched, suggesting Mary's robes were immodest. Mary adorned herself in a catastrophe of robes and hair, liquorice and flung back from her face. She wore her face mostly bare, except smudges of charcoal on her eyelids, her mouth paintless though still tinged crimson, I thought in my unworldly mind, from the abrasion of men's mouths.

And when she comes here now, having dragged her sex across roads, road worker's hands, cotton sheets, silk, bare mattresses, across angry fingers and sharpened teeth, across clumsy shaking thighs, I want to smell every sediment smell there, but can't. I have barely moved in all these millennia, but she has ridden horses where they want to go, hankered and hunkered down in alleys and cars, turned men face down on beds and left them to reassemble, limbs bruised and disquieted. She is filthy with stories and I wish I could smell her reek. And this man in blue, lost, a fist of fishhooks she dragged across this ancient seabed to me.


**HE CLIMBS THE** bluff's stones and dirt, climbs, pauses, breath stolen, the slope extending further still. He turns and looks out towards the horizon. Sand. More sand. He hoped he might see the road from here. A blue smudge on the horizon to the

east might be the Red Sea. But it could be merely moisture or
dew rising from the sands as the day warms. Dizzy, stomach
complaining, he wonders if he is hungry in the moment before
he feels famished. He staggers one foot, then the next, lungs
despairing the height of the climb. Sees the edge of the crest.
Wills himself to stagger past the burning muscles in his legs,
the swoon.

This is not like the other bluffs. From the highest point,
where he now stands, it slopes gently down the other side, a
handful of gnarled and confused trees, a few shacks, even a
well at the bottom edge of the slope. Nowhere. Not a village.
Maybe once, but no one lives here now. No fires and none of
the bustling activity required to live in the desert like this.
He lurches forward. Wonders if she was leading him here, but
the abandoned buildings seem empty. Silence pools among the
hovels and discarded pots. He has been led astray by a ghost who
has drawn him here like a tongue to a canker sore.


**WAITING IS EROSION**, finds itself where the callous sky abrades
the sand dunes, torqued innocents on a sprawling bed. Years
became a handful of stones, months just dust, and sunsets and
sunrises flared by, so I shut my eyes and left them to their stut-
tering. I lost count.

It seems I can't die. There isn't even that to wait for.

I walked here, after he dredged me up from the stench of my
own rot, back from the dead. I stayed with my sister Mary for
perhaps a month. But there were too many questions. The desert
promised fewer.

Weeks later, my sisters stumbled here too. Sent by my mother,
and though they feared the hills, the bare darkness and cries
of foxes, the winds that smother, they were more afraid of our

mother, who Mary says won't leave the kitchen table where she weeps and pushes off the table any dish with food Mary or Martha put in front of her. For my mother I was already dead in some way. My sisters told me how she had mourned. Closed all the windows, blacked out the world. Spent most of her days angry at him for making her mourn her loss twice. She said to Mary before she later died, "It's a terrible and unnatural thing for a mother to die knowing the corpse of her son lives on." I laughed when Mary told me. She said I was unkind.

And so my sisters made rituals to keep themselves busy. But I required so little care since I never ate, never shit nor pissed. They wandered around me searching for tasks, sweeping the steps, washing the floors of the hovels, washing my feet, my hands. My flesh would not heal, would not cease to stink, no matter if they washed or not, so they no longer went further than my hands or feet. I ceased to speak, so they had only the company of each other, and they had never cared for each other's company much. So they knitted together an anger towards me.

In the days after he raised me from the dead, Mary boasted he did it out of love for her, because of her pleading. Later, here in the desert, her pride turned to a rancid burden. Her begging had gotten her a brother who was a corpse. "He was a fool," she lashed more than once. "He should have let you die," writing herself out of the story.

He did. He just didn't let me stay that way. Couldn't leave well enough alone.

"What about his work? The Lord's work?" she'd asked on her more charitable days.

I couldn't bring myself to tell them, to explain. They coveted their faith; they believed in him devoutly. Tempting, a night here or there where I would despair at this ache and waiting, tempting to think of taking away that faith, of telling them. Then we could sit here in the desert together, each silenced. But they were kind, my sisters. Kinder than me.

I think Mary could tell I was pulling away, my answers to her questions fewer and further between. She soon sensed it was pointless.

Then, months after they had followed me there, she sat with me one night, the purpling of the rock ridges, the dunes, the sky washing away, and in her silence a new resignation.

"We should leave," something cracked open in her vocal chords. "We're leaving," as though she were conjugating this verb for the first time. Our younger sister had wanted to leave months before, never fully understanding what had happened to me or why they had followed me here. "What should we tell mother?" No pleading or guilt in her voice now, just uncertainty.

I spoke then. For the last time. Instructed her to tell our mother that I had died once more. At last. And to promise her I would not rise again.

She nodded. Then the two of us rested on the bluff looking out over the desert as it swallowed itself.

Years later Martha returned to tell me of our mother's death. She could not stay long. She watched our mother's body gripped to the black hem of her grave dress, hoping it would not rise, hoping that if it did she could somehow hold it down. She longed for a simple grief and, this time, she got it.

One day Mary touched my hand. I raised my eyes to hers, flushes of cerulean pain. She leaned crumpled, creased in front of me, the years eroding her, to tell me of Martha's death. She added that she would not return. No grey-washed husband or unkind children to tell me of her death when it would come, so when the flies replaced her I exhaled one last time, the days thinning out in front of me.

My lovely sisters, in the months of their waiting, made mud and straw into hovels, for them and for me, to hide me from the sun or those who would gawk. But I liked better the open yard, preferred this simple stone wall burnt by the sun, the sand-grit wind, watching this dust swirl past my feet. I am not really alone. Foxes calling foxes, the laziness of cobras, the blue-headed lizards and the weary storks on their wilful migration. Yes, wanderers used to come too. People other than the Marys. Seeking a seer, an oracle, a guru. I did nothing and my silence and distance from the world made these few believe me to be a prophet. I said nothing to dissuade them.

And I looked like no man, my body in pieces barely held together. If a thousand birds tore the flesh from this rack and scattered on these diseased winds to the corners of this planet, would I still feel every piece? A desire covering the whole world. The faithful priests took their forsaken, the leprous, and named them my children. Stranded them on islands. Sealed them in windowless hospitals. I'm sure my sisters would point out that this isn't any way to celebrate a miracle. Yet they could never admit that, not for a second. That their saviour might have made a mistake.

I can't say when it was, how long after Mary last left, that this woman with the already written body came to me. She seemed a part of the hills, a piece of sky staggering at my feet at my feet bleeding blue. A blue robe, a simple chair she set beside mine, perhaps the same waiting stare slowly scanning the desert. We sat under a hundred suns before she nodded, with the lumbering slowness of mountains crumbling under glaciers. We could see the longing in each other, salt washed and thin. Familiar.

Then she left. For a thousand years. Until now. Now she brings him. This small critter, hankering after her into the desert.

**HE LEANS OVER THE WELL**, pulls up the rope and finds the bucket full of clear water. Holds it up to his face and gulps in fierce mouthfuls. Parasites be damned. He shucks his shirt fast, splashes water all over his chest. He collapses there, in the mud made by the water smattering on the dirt, and his chest heaves and he is so glad to not have to walk another step. He will drink all the water in the well and then he will die here if he must, but he will not go another step.

**THE ABSURDITY OF IT**. He has the same long neck. The same long latitude of muscles running down his torso, the ribs running corrugated, disappearing under muscle. His hair is a golden colour, almost copper, not the same coarse black that the man we knew had, but it doesn't distract. She is cruel. She brought him here to remind me. My mouth wet for the first time in a millennium. And I can imagine his scent. How his mother fed him nothing but fish and rice each day, and so now he tastes saltier than others. And how he eats sweet things, chocolate, drinks colas, syrup, hoping he can sugar down the salty.

And yet it must have tortured this woman to bring him here, this souvenir. I hope she is tortured by this. He scuffs the dirt, lost, maybe ten feet from me. Ten feet from seeing me, monstrous and leprous. Beg the flies to rest in their buzzing, so that he might not notice me. So that I can see him just a little longer. I long for him to move more slowly, to give each moment more gravity. I have been careless with time, disregarded it, and now, a stitch in the ribs, pained as it blows past and on to the sea, I want to cling to it, hold it here to languish, one more glimpse of him.

She did this. I will not forgive her.

I wish I could smell, even for just a moment, to see if this man smells like him, the one she and I have both tried to forget. Lime pulp on lips, he liked to chew limes. Warm smell of dried mint between his fingers, an olive's saltiness on his neck below his ear, the wood dust caught in the hairs of his forearms.

The warehouse on the south side of the city where they stored the unsold furniture they had built. I had gone with him to find a chair a cotton merchant wanted for his mother. Late afternoon, he unlocked the warehouse and led me in among the sleeping mountains of unused furniture. Dark circles under his eyes, that precipice look, he stood gazing out over the furniture like he was trying to remember why we were there. A light red tinge limned his eyes; he had been crying. He was crying more each day and when I asked him why, he said he was trying to feel it all. I don't know what that meant.

In all our friendship I had not supposed anything, had not reached for him, not asked for or made any gesture or declaration of love. I accepted his kisses on the crown of my head as he passed me in the backyard on the way to pick olives. I accepted when he leaned against me or held my hand in the busy market street, under the looming mountains as the sun fell behind, the shadows drawing us down into the lake water. But I had never kissed him or reached for him. I could not. And he knew why. I think he knew why.

But that afternoon I took his hand. He turned away from the bone church of chairs. Such sadness in his eyes. He did not hide it from me. Words scattering under furniture before I could say them, so I led him to a bed frame, removed stacked chairs from on top of it, and drew him down beside me on the slats. Chest to back, holding him from behind, my face lightly pressed against the nape of his neck, as though I was for hours in the middle of a kiss. I remember that one unending kiss as a tether, that I held him to the afternoon in the warehouse on the edge of the city, held him, like I already knew he was leaving or that I soon would. In the diminishing light our breaths rose up and fell, waves submitted to the tide, my chest to his back ribs and his back ribs to my chest, pressed to the ebbing warmth in among the sleeping ribs of furniture.

**THE SUN MORE CONFIDENT** overhead now, his bare chest and face start to sear. He needs shelter. He stumbles to one of the huts, pushes the door open, finds a bed. He lies down on the old mattress. Falls into feverish dreams of blood clotting in the gutter.

**I WATCH HIM** pull himself into the hovel, wanting him to find shelter but also wanting to go on seeing him, his wet back, sodden face, then heaving chest there in the dirt. Not gone. That hut where the Marys used to sleep.

She's gone, has abandoned him.

How long ago was the last Mary here. No food could have lasted this long. There is nothing to feed him.

Then I feel her. She is a bad wind from the sea. The olive tree and the bushes along the west wall rustle anxiously. A henna grief spreads from her hands, up her arms, across her scapulas and licks her neck. This man she brought to cause me pain, is causing her pain.

**ERIC SLIPS IN AND OUT** of sleep. Drowsiness infects the day. He's sick. He feels sick. Maybe from the hunger. He remembers a summer when he was fifteen, the daughter of the family that ran the fish and chip place down at the dock by the bay. Her long, apricot hair, her downturned mouth, her perfect obliviousness. He'd slouched around all that summer as though desire was a great burden. The drowsy flies in the shade of the hut seem to feel longing too. A great beast is swallowing him. Its sad, long throat cinching him down. Then sleep drowns him again.

**SHE PERCHES BESIDE ME** on the low wall that circles the hovels. The wall is too low to keep sand or critters in or out, but it is just the right height for sitting. If I could still smell, I'd smell jasmine, cardamom, lemons. In her room she always kept a bowl of lemons on her bedside table. She claimed they protected her. Between the men, she'd sometimes hold a lemon up to her nose, press her lips against it. Sunshine for those days she spent in the dust shadows. She told me all this once, in a moment of generosity. Before she knew about him and me.

Her robes billow, a flap, then a day or two of stillness, quiet, perhaps even the folds of sighing, sleepy after all this wandering.

"I sent them to you."

"All of them?"

"Yes."

"Like postcards."

"Yes. So you would know. In Tripoli, in Thesilonika, in Belgrave, in Montreal and Sumatra. I remembered you."

"I didn't know. But why?"

She looks to the east. Once again, we are strangers here.

I want to ask why she has brought him, this man baited into the desert. I am afraid the words will fall out, grain flowing from a torn sack.

"Did you see his waist?" she asks. The dimples at the base of his spine.

"No," I lie.

"When I saw him in Dahab, I noticed the narrow waist. Those vee lines, plunging down. Familiar."

"I didn't notice."

"And that long neck. Unnaturally long. Like a woman's."

She has turned towards me a little; she studies my face for a slip, a crack of desire. But I have sat here through wars, through sand storms, through the barrage of days and the insistent flurry of Marys' hands. I can still temper these resurrected feelings. Though they broil and turn in my gut.

A flash of memory: she leans over me, a wide grin, river water dripping from her face her neck, dropping all over my skin where I lie in the sun. She's laughing, waking me from my nap. A flash of what she must have looked like as a little girl, I see her eyes are washed clean of the kohl, and here in the sepia light, her eyes are stained brown, brown tea, not the glaring black she wears in the market and the women's den.

This was before she knew I loved him, that he might love me, but the summer when she had figured out I would not try to lie with her, run my hands over her. The two of us without him, at the river, in the market, playacting that we were more than our desire for him. In that small time, there was a sudden peace between us, and I saw a face on her I hadn't seen before and wouldn't see again. No pocket-knife defiance, no grit-molar defence, she was a different woman. A girl, even, running from the river to cascade cool water drops on my burnished sleepy skin, the river shattering light around the dirge of her laugh as she pinned me under her.

"Can you smell that?" her pebbled voice dragging me back to the desert.

"What?" I humour her.

"Him. His reek."

"No."

"Maybe peaches. And pepper."

"You can smell him from here?"

"I could smell him from Cairo. From Barcelona maybe, if I

wanted to. I trust how a man smells. But peaches. His mother feeds him peaches that have been pitted, cut, syruped, and placed in a metal container on dusty shelves."

"Peaches and pepper."

"Cardamom. The kind of man who never kisses a woman first."

"Why did he follow you here?"

"Because I wanted him to."

"And what now?"

She leans her head a little towards him, a despairing smile breaking across her face.

A small moment. The night after the slat bed. In the market, a man taunted him, threw an orange and hit him in the chest so the three of us fled, an erratic confusion of back alleys, and as we hid in a doorway, he leaned into me, his temple pressed to my chest. She glanced back from the alley, half wild defensive creature, half laughing girl thrilled with the game, a moment as small as a breath and as sudden as a wall in the dark. She looked me clearly in the eyes, intently. He had never been soft belly like this with her. We both loved him secretly, but now she was on uneven footing. She stood alone with her longing.

I see her there in the fading light of the desert. Alone. I can't know how she wants this to end, but I can see why now. She is here for him. For the dust and bones that might end this longing that has left us to haunt and wander.

HE WAKES SLOWLY, aware first of the heat-drunk buzz of flies, the smell of sunshine cracking its way under the hovel door. Then, the tearing pangs of hunger. He hasn't eaten in twenty-four hours. At least he's not lost in the desert. Though he might as well be. Longing still shoulders its weight, holding him to this desolate bed. No matter. He is still alone.

He wonders, idly, if the woman means for him to follow her further. A headache needles in the corners of his eyes.

He decides to drink more water. Just something in his stomach so he can stave off the hunger. He staggers up, limbs weighed down as if the air is water. Stays barefoot, tired of the binding shoes. Opens the door to the blaring light, stands, eyes closed, face and feet bare to the surface of the sun. Blink, blinks his eyes, trying to focus in the glare.

He hears the buzz of the frustrated flies boiling the air. Under the tree, in the shade, two people sitting as still as corpses. The woman with the gory robes, still life and watching him. Beside her, taller, yet crooked, like a tree grown against a stone wall, looms another figure.

She rises. She steps out from the shade, out from under the tree. She takes a long stride, pauses, another, like she is blind and only taking each step after she is certain of the next. Her hooded head tilts; she smells her way around him. He wants to step back. And she takes another stride, maybe only a few metres between them now.

She stops. Her robes billow in currents, the stream running on without her. She is river stones. He should say something. That figure still sits back by the tree, has turned its head ever so slightly, angled now to watch the two of them. And they all three hang celestial, waiting for gravity.


IF I COULD SMELL, I know I would smell her stench of the departed sea, the wreckage of seaweed and shattered shells. This long lost smell of caramel and dried onions on her fingers. And the lemons. She still hungers. She moves to him all mouth and teeth. I fear she will swallow him in one gulp. But she pauses. Does she want him, or does she want me to want him?

Tired of waiting for the one we both longed for, she's arranged this little play within a play. But she doesn't know how it ends.

He's afraid. I can see in frantic glances, how his chest heaves like the breath of a rabbit in one's hands, can see a vein pulse in his long neck. He's just a boy. In this she's failed. We are both older than god, and this little pet, as familiar as he is, truly can only remind us both of all the time since we last saw the man who left us to our longing. We are ancient and decaying. He, she says, smells of peaches and cardamom. Strange, how I can remember what peaches or cardamom smell like. How I can feel the sap in the olive tree stir now, as dead as it is. Which Mary planted it, I can't remember.

The two of them metres apart between here and the hovels. He grows thinner by the moment, as transparent as rice paper, organs vivid and legible. She who laid under and upon a thousand men, slick with their sweat, rank, her hair torturous knots tangled on that rough bed. She is marble steps worn into recesses, collecting rain. She is leather worn smooth then rough again. She is beaches beaten and torn out with the undertow. She hankers for the small measure of wear each man brings her, how she abrades them in turn. But she circles him, wearing more teeth than usual. Incisors and molars.

Blood flows in stabs into these charcoal limbs, wood flushing into flesh after centuries. Her plan cutting into my temples clearly, to make me feel again so she can make me suffer. She gives so she can take away. He doesn't stand a chance.

**THE THUMPING OF HIS** own heart buries Eric. He feels certain she can feel the thick pulses in the air all those feet away. Specks of light hang in his periphery, the sun setting him slowly afire, she bleeds into the air around her, her robes billowing slightly, coiled. And he's afraid, but the fear has no hold, no musculature.

He takes a step forward, like she's cursed him to do it. A fraction of a moment before his step touches the ground she steps away.

Another step, and she flashes further back. He feels thick blood bloom up his neck to his head. Thinks he can lead this tango.

Then she strides a sudden step forward, he falters, face suddenly pale milk — he takes a step back, reflexively. No telling whose tango it is. Their limbs caught in the same trap. She must have some plan. She led him here in the first place. He hazards a look at the figure back under the tree; it has tilted its head back to look up through the branches at the sky, face exposed. Bandages wrapped around that face, mummified. In that moment, he sees the webs around him, her waiting to pounce. Grasps he's been caught all along.

**SHE HANGS OVER ME**, carrion urges holding her. She's wrought more for wrecking than pleasing. She flinches, tilting her head back, runs her eyes down this dusty form, reads my slumped shoulders, the lean to my crumbling form, the way she can read all men, even one as hollow-husked as me.

She lurches towards the north, towards the downward slope, but then hurtles up behind him before he can turn his head. Her hands reach from behind, meet at his clavicles, and she tears his shirt off. He staggers, and she tastes this, knocks him sideways so he falls to the ground. She has tied his arms behind him and bound him to himself before he can raise himself up.

His bare chest heaving, shocked, the deference of prey, his long neck thick, thick with blood, his head thrown back and twisting to see. Even a vein in his forehead pulses now. So much blood. He is near bursting with blood, this small universe called a man.

She steps back, as though presenting him, her mouth grimacing, joyful in her pain like she might pass this disease to me. She can see my head has turned towards him, can hear something almost like breath rattling through me. She wants to see me suffer. The way only desire can make one suffer. She is the cruellest pestilence. Wish I had strength to crush her throat; the dust on his collarbone, the rhythm of his heaving chest, the sweat on his forehead, saliva in the corner of his dry lips. Cruel.

But still I don't tell her the secret of that olive tree. A secret that would have her fall to grey dust. Hold the words. Don't tell her how I collected his body in a grain sack, brought it here. Stayed with him, making sure he did not rise, or that if he did he would not be left alone. Like me.

SHE RUNS A BARBED WIRE HAND across Eric's chest. She has him bound and shirtless. She holds him to the collapsing figure like a caught prize. Fear rises up his spine, an arctic drowning water.

She hasn't bathed in months, has covered her sinewy skin in strong scents, cinnamon, lavender, and none of it covers the tar stench reeking out from under her robe.

The corpse man looks at first like he's falling. Her hand freezes on Eric's chest, the nails digging in a little deeper, but caught. Then, the corpse pushes up, gripping a contorted stick in one hand, leans and stoops slowly up. Dust and sand pour off his lap to the ground around his feet. All the while her nails stay dug into Eric's chest flesh. They are both breathless, watching the corpse.

He staggers a step, then two, then leans against the trunk of the tree.

She stirs behind Eric, a nest of serpents lash coiled and now squint-eyed. She pushes hard between his shoulder blades so his face and chest press down into the sand. Her hands are quick as furies. His belt is gone, unlashed. He struggles, but she holds him planted in the dirt. She tears his pants from him, cotton shredding, then his blue plaid boxers. And he is naked in the courtyard, bare, white to the desert sky.

She releases the pressure on his back. He struggles to torque his head off the ground, lurches to see. The bucket clanks against itself and grinds the stones that line the well. With a thud she comes down on his back again, shoving his face in the dirt. She dumps the bucket all over his head, his back, his legs, soaks the dirt around him to mud. Buzz of the flies, he struggles to angle his head so he can see. The corpse man still leans against the tree, but has turned his head towards them. Taste of blood and dirt, Eric sees clearly this man can't save him.

Her colic laugh behind him, then the searing sting, he throws his head back, as she runs her barbed hands from the nape of his neck down his back ribs, down to the small of his back, across his ass, and down his legs. Pain replaces the fear, and he drops his face back to the dirt. Warm, solid, the ground reassures him. The pain is nothing to this dirt, the stone walls, the ancient tree aching for the blind sky.

**THE MAN WE LOVED**, his hands were soft, tiny. You wouldn't know he worked with them. I remember his hands in his lap as he sat across from me in my mother's yard. He was not disgusted, not sickened by my rotted flesh, the disease about me, and this somehow made my condition worse. I could have borne him not looking at me, eyes averted, but he looked right at me, right into my eyes, so I averted mine.

I could tell he didn't have much longer. My sister brought us olives, some cheese, bread, tea and I watched how he would even bring each olive, each fig to his mouth like he had never tasted it before. When it was time to leave, he stood, stepped towards where I sat, and it occurred to me he was going to try to kiss me. And that kiss, the way he would kiss my cheek, my forehead. But I could not tolerate him that close to the rot stench of me. Even as I remembered the taste of his mouth, on my lips, the warmth as he laid in my arms in the carpenter's warehouse, I told him he must leave.

She strokes this naked man she has pressed down into the mud, wet, like some first man rising up from creation. He is nothing like us, no reek of hunger, no mouth gone septic. Obscenely far away. Fragile. Beauteous. If I press my face to the small of his back, or the nape of his neck, might my sense of smell return? Or at least I could rest my bandaged cheek there, sleep a little. I miss sleep, that space outside dreams where the mind falls off the edge, free of insect thoughts. I could sleep now. The small rhythm of his breath pressing into his back ribs, the warmth of him, cooler than the sun. How skin sticks to skin in the desert. I could sleep.

She scalpels her nails up his back ribs, spine, raw red welts the length of him. Her laugh like branches shattering against branches, birds being beaten against the stones of riverbeds. And I feel the wetness on my chest. I am crying.

PAIN LASHES IN LINES down his back, the sun burning, blistering his bare skin. She has him pinned tight to the earth. She is a chainsaw's chain derailed, she is cables snapped, her claws tearing at his already tattered back.

Across the courtyard, the corpse weeps and slides down the bark of the tree.

Wet tickle of blood running from the torn skin. He struggles, but she pins him tighter.

Then the corpse speaks. Eric strains to hear past the agony, contorts to crane his neck towards where the corpse slumps against the tree. The words are not French. Maybe Arabic. He can't tell. But the woman loosens her grip.

The man speaks again, then struggles, braces against the tree to stand again. Then he presses his face to the bark. Like he's kissing it.

He hears her let out a wail, a funeral dirge with ground glass and the cries of small mortal creatures. And then she releases him. The corpse man staggers back from the tree.

Eric rolls over. The woman's robes are flung wide, her famished face, covered in rouge and powder, a parody of a woman. A crack of light in her eyes, she glares at the corpse figure, now disregarding Eric. Despite the burning and bleeding wounds on his back, he forces himself to roll clear of her, then, his hands still bound, shoulders to his knees, staggers to his feet, then to the nearest hovel, and throws himself on the dirt floor.

But she does not even look in his direction. She is billowed, sprung, a storm cloud of pooling blood in the air above his own blood speckled in the mud.

The corpse man staggers away from the tree.

Her robes shudder, snap of cloth in the air, a mere blink and she has flung herself against the trunk with a thundering smack, bark chips flying, the branches shaking in reply.

She backs up, then flies against the tree again.

Then she is a flurry at the roots of the tree, sand flying, chips of bark.

The man backs further away, then slumps down where he

started, back into the slumbering rest of his past death, not watching the woman, like he knows how this will end.

She flings the sand into the air, a sand storm carrying out over the desert. Her robes tear where they fall between her and the tree. Scraps of the red fabric snow down around the hovels.

She wails, reaches down, grabs two of the largest exposed roots. The tree, massive, shudders as the roots tear from the sand and dirt. Tributary roots, the tree's underground system of veins and vessels tear into the light. It crashes to the ground in a thunder crack of broken limbs and a great cloud of sand. She ululates, the cries of the Bedouin women in far off villages joining her, shaking the hovels and sending lightning cracks through the stones. She teeters, her hands swooning to the ground, sliding under, hefting the rag-swaddled figure gently from the earth.

She lifts the bundle, still ululating, berates the sun, now uncertain in the west. She turns to the corpse man, holds the bundle towards him, the wailing sinking to a growl. Then to a wail again. She slumps to one knee, leaning the figure against her and with her free hand, tentative with ache, parts the fabric, reveals a skeleton. The howls fade, grief beyond sound. She touches the forehead of the skeleton, but the skull collapses into dust, the frame of bones falling from her hold. With that, in the fist of a fresh grief and a pyrrhic longing, she wraps the sackcloth around the shattered bones. She stands. Her tattered robes billow around her again, she pulls her hood forward, sheltering her face from the light. She hovers there, then turns toward the corpse man. He sits as he sat before. Like he's always known.

Eric cowers, naked, in the shade of the hovel, imagines fleeing, running across the sands to the seam of road that could take him to Cairo, but can't bring himself to move, a starling with a mangled wing in the dust among immortals, waiting for the end.

**IN THE RECESS LEFT BEHIND** by the roots she finds his bones, dishevelled by the tree as it grew over him. She stands over the grave, a wail lashing out of her. She knew him marrow deep, can smell him now. It seems foolish to me, how I let her go on wandering, my greedy heart and the selfishness of the olive tree.

She turns to me then, all jagged edges. I see she will destroy every atom of me. Or I will become air. And she will not rest until then. I can see all this in the creased wrought grief of her face.

A knife slides through her anger, her fierceness focuses into a blade's point.

She turns to the hovel, turns to where the gentle hands man cowers, then she looks at me. I take in a small breath, as though to make a noise, as though to stop her, but she smirks then, and I see I have given her resolve.

She strides into the shelter, then drags the naked man out kicking, hollering for help, trying to turn to me, to get my mercy.

With one hand she grabs his hair, pulls back his head and he whimpers, and then with the other hand she gouges her nails into the flesh, tears the pulsing meat of his neck, shucking clam from shell, tears the veins so blood splatters, flung brown and muddy around them. His beautiful, jerking body hangs from her, ornamental and broken.

She knows it's a small gesture. But she makes me suffer. She came back for this.

She releases the body into the bloody mud, glances down at him as he shudders, seeping into the earth.

I close my eyes. Maybe now sleep. Maybe in the pieces and the scattering a possible nothingness even.

I hear her now, in the olive grave, her jagged grief, her whispers to the bundle she has made.

I can't hear her.

I open my eyes. And she is gone from the hill, the sky, the desert. Here I sit, next to the wreckage of the olive tree. With the slowness of weeks, I slide to my knees, unbind his hands. With water from the well, I wash the young man clean of his blood. And I push him in the open grave the tree's sprung roots have offered beside the bundle of bones. Push dirt over his delicate skin and crumpled form, over the two of them. And for days I lie, my dry, bandaged cheek on the mound of dirt. I wait for another Mary to come. I know she will send one in time. The winds pick up, blowing sand over me, the dunes from the south cresting and pressing in to drown me years from now. On another continent, this boy's mother sleeps, his t-shirt under her pillow, grief traveling to her, but for now she sleeps for us both and I hold his body down in the soil, praying he will not rise, wishing I was down there with him.

# CARE

# CARE

MORGAN SOBS, hides her face in her hands, sobs some more and peeks through her fingers at the med student who uncrosses his legs, then crosses them the other way, worrying the folder in front of him. He scribbles something, a doubtful wince creasing the corner of his left eye. His cheeks flush an apple shyness that doesn't match the fauxhawk hair, the excessive tanning. He doesn't look half as tired as a good med student should, she thinks. He's not asked another question since the scribble so Morgan assumes he's now just making random notes to buy time until he can remember what to do next. She's not going to help him.

Fauxhawk somehow passed all those years of post-secondary. A person in authority gave him that file folder, that white coat. Now he should help her. Or maybe he should go no further.

The doctor monitoring the practice squints at his clipboard, but Morgan sees the ruse in his bouncing left knee, how he reaches out and presses the clipboard, a cover to hide his smartphone.

The med student clears his throat, scratches down another small note. Morgan wishes she could see what he's writing. Probably "ohshitohshitohshit." Poor guy.

Maybe he wants to be a plastic surgeon. Maybe nowhere in the medical program material did they mention a woman like her, sobs like hers, a day like this.

"Can I just get something for the pain?" she asks for the third time. The med student squints up from his folder.

"And you said you got these bruises from a fall?"

"Yes."

"And where did you fall again?"

"The living room."

You didn't write it down in your folder, Morgan quips to herself. Things she can't say off script. The guy should be better prepared, should be solving the problem not burying her under repetitive questions.

"I've been really tired. Exhausted," she prods him.

The med student squints at her. "Do you have a well-balanced diet?" he asks, but it goes up a little too much on the end like he's questioning the question.

Not what you're supposed to ask, thinks Morgan. Moron. Give her the coat and the file folder and she could out-diagnose him and actually care for a weeping woman.

"I'm sorry. There's just some routine questions I have to ask."

"For what?"

"To make sure that you're . . . okay."

"Okay." She takes a breath. "As I said, I'm tired. I'm not getting any sleep." And still he looks half twitchy, half lost. She's given him almost every prompt.

She sneezes.

He holds the pen over the file, still with desperation.

"Disregard the sneeze. Not relevant," the monitoring doctor whispers to the med student.

Morgan tries not to roll her eyes. Disregard the eye rolling. Not relevant.

The med student leans back in his seat, jostles an underused synapse which accidentally fires and he almost lunges forward in his chair. "Has anyone at home ever hit or touched you in a violent way?"

Morgan realizes she has to actually answer his question. But she doesn't want to give him the satisfaction of getting it right, finding the relevant question after all his fumbling.

"Yes," she says. He's on the edge of the chair now, eyes wide and the corners of his mouth giddy to slip into a smile, like he just scored a point, and she wants to punch him right in the face. Kapow. That would train him to respond to a woman being beaten in a more appropriate fashion. The Standardized Patient training manual does not indicate excitement as an appropriate response.

He leans further in his seat, cocky now. "Well, you do realize this is very serious, don't you," he says, nodding gravely, and he can't help himself, sneaks a smug look at the monitoring doctor expecting approval. Now Morgan really wants to punch him.

The Standardized Patient training made an art out of repetition. Five of them struggled in that session, each playing out the same scenario, rehearsing the symptoms, the same lament, the same request for pain killers. The same resistance to answering the med student's questions. By the end, the five actors had algorithmed the necessary symptoms and emotions. Proficient human problems to be solved. That woman Ava though, the new girl, she made sickness an art. She had the benefit of a downturned mouth, so that when she looked at the floor trying to avoid the doctor's gaze her whole face begged for mercy. Morgan hated her own perky little poppy mouth, more round than long and no sad turn or happy turn. Mostly unremarkable. Ava's mouth confused others, left them often uncertain of how she was feeling. A non-committal mouth, good for moments of deliberation, poker, and first dates, but, she felt, it also held her back as an actress. But this Ava, her mouth played every pathos perfectly. She should only ever play beaten, downtrodden women or depressives.

When they paused for coffee, Morgan brought her a chocolate chip cookie. "You're really good," she whispered, not wanting the other actresses to hear a compliment, not wanting to send them into a tizzy of wondering why they didn't get one too.

"Thanks," she said, taking the cookie from her and then taking a bite. Not even the cookie made her lose pathos. Such a beautiful sadness.

"I'm Morgan."

"Ava."

Morgan couldn't help herself from wondering if anything could surpass this mouth: was it like this when she was tickled, did it still pull down at the sides during sex, did the heavy mouth even sandbag her laugh. Had the mouth started off just wide and horizontal, only to sink, weighed down by pain and selfish men? Maybe the mouth first drew itself this way in the womb, now endured all these mistaken readings, pathetic fallacy of the mouth. Not things one can ask over a cookie. But Morgan couldn't help wanting a mouth just like that. One day.

Not like Morgan's mouth hasn't known adversity. When she was five, she leapt from a playground jungle gym to grab a zip line handle and her foot hooked around one of the railing bars. She fell three feet face first into the ground. When she seized up from the ground, wailing, a gap stood where her loose front tooth had dangled. Her mother had to dig around in the dirt to find it. She cried for what must have been hours, but her mother never stopped holding her.

"Did you fall?" her mother asked in a calming whisper.

"Yeeeaaaahhhh," she wailed back between sobs.

Morgan remembers pain. Jagged stabs of pain where her mouth hit the ground, but the fierceness of her mother's hug upstaged it, as though she believed her crushing arms could squeeze the pain out of her daughter. In Morgan's memory, the gritty taste of the playground sand, her tears splattering the copper and leaf-green speckled sunlight, and the taste of her mother's soap clean neck all wash together into the perfect care.

Last Christmas Eve, her mother, three rum and diet cokes into the evening, added an appendix to the story. The story itself had circulated and been retold at various family events, perhaps because it seemed so emblematic of what her mother and aunts thought of as Morgan's brash and ill-fated leaps in life. That night, though, her mother confessed in a kitchen aside that if she hadn't been crying a little herself about all the late nights Morgan's father worked, then maybe she would have seen the monkey bar events unfolding. Maybe she could have caught Morgan. She as good as pushed her child off the jungle gym and knocked out that front tooth. Morgan stared at her mother and took a gulp of her eggnog and rum, certain her mother wasn't so much feeling bad about the event as she just wanted to be told she was a good mother. Two drunk aunts returned to the kitchen and saved Morgan from that forced testimony.

Edward, her boyfriend, could never be mistaken for a story-book love interest. No Heathcliff or Mr. Darcy. A moderate man. She has never seen him angry, or crying, and he laughs like a contortion, no sound coming out. And that makes him in so many ways the perfect man for her. Except when she gets a cold or the flu, and then she realizes he has no sense or taste for comforting. The happy, she thinks, have no need for comforting. The first couple of times she got sick in their relationship she found herself angry at him because he didn't coddle her, make homemade vegetarian chicken noodle soup, didn't plump up his bottom lip and give her a look of poor you. Mostly he pedaled off on his weird bike with no brakes and collected driftwood at the beach that he planned to make into various derelict pieces of furniture, but then just piled in the corner of the living room, a growing art installation symbolizing his neglect and lack of commitment to art and her. He saw no point in both of them getting sick — sensible. He's sensible. And most of the time she finds that comforting.

"I'm Jane Eaton and I'm a second year med student. I'll be talking to you before you go in to see the doctor." This next med student, a woman, perches grimly intent on getting this right. Strands of hair asymmetrically escape her attempt at polish and professionalism, so she has the allure of a slow collapse. She has woodchucked the end of her pencil with anxiety. Morgan wants to help her, a ragged itch under her rib cage. But maybe she won't need help.

"Can you tell me a little about why you're here today," the med student asks, then leans in towards Morgan a little more. Maybe she means to look comforting, but it feels a little more vulturous. Morgan leans back from the doctor, a small escape. The doctor clues in and leans back herself.

"I fell. Between the living room and the dining room. Lip of the carpet."

"Your injuries don't signify a fall though. It says here symptoms are . . . oh shit, I should be talking to you, not about you."

Morgan blinks, not stepping out of the scenario. She has to keep the doctor going.

The med student takes her lead. "Your injuries look like you had more than a fall." She places the patient file on the floor next to the chair and folds one hand into the other to give her hands something to do while she holds Morgan in her gaze.

"Can you tell me, has anyone ever hit you?"

"What are you getting at? I told you. I fell."

"I am required to ask you a series of questions. They are completely routine, but the hospital requires I ask them. Nothing personal."

"I just want something for the pain."

"Well, I am not a pharmacist. I am someone who tries to deal with the problem, not just the symptom."

Morgan's eyes want to cross and roll back at the same time. She hides this by putting her face in her hands, and letting out a fake sob. She's overplaying the emotion but it feels good. Feels really good. Been a while since she's had a good cry. Ava might be good at the forlorn downtrodden thing, but crying did not come easily for her in the training sessions. Morgan, though, could Meryl Streep the hell out of tears. Round noncommittal mouth be damned, she could put it to purpose with a good cry, make the bottom lip tremble and shudder with a wailing distress.

Behind the tears, she feels a small itch of guilt for hauling out the weeping; emotions take time, swallow up the med student's chance to get this right. After the eye-crossing-rolling moment, Morgan felt compelled to help the student fail. A little payback for the patronizing speech she'd given. Who patronizes a beaten woman? Ludicrous.

"It's okay," the med student says to her.

And Morgan wants to yell back, I've been beaten by my husband and now a lame ass med student is patronizing me. What makes this okay?

The student blanches, looks to the corners of the room like they might be hiding what to do next. Scans her notes looking for an exit.

"Can you tell me a little more about what brought you here today?" She looks back up.

Seriously. They've gone back that far in the questions. The med student is going to run out of time. The buzzer will go before she can even get Morgan to admit to the domestic violence. Morgan has to gather in her sobs then, give herself a moment to stop feeling impatient, stop thinking about the buzzer, stop being angry with the med student's patronizing tone so she can be what this woman, this character is, feel what she feels in this moment. Free from Morgan's experience of this tedious, clumsy minded med student.

In the training they had explained why they used actors. Because actors could disassociate. Could follow a script and an emotional reality without one compromising the other.

The buzzer bleats. The med student's face collapses. Morgan feels a little bad. Maybe she could have offered herself up a little more, paper lantern to the student's questions. She had indulged more emotionally than the script necessitated; guilt glanced back to that impulse, her desire to make the student fail.

She wonders after Ava, wonders how Ava's students fared. How could they have any emotional distance from that mouth? How did they not just lean in and hold her? How do they not just give her prescriptions for everything she wants and needs? How do they not utterly forget the fiction of the simulation and just see a damaged and torn woman?

Morgan, despite others sometimes perceiving her as cold, would give a patient like Ava everything. When she was eight, she snuck money from her mother's purse, a full twenty dollars. She spent it all on junk food she took over to their babysitter's house. Tanya B. A high school cheerleader whose parents made her work for the money she spent on cotton-candy lip gloss, fuchsia scrunchies and her trademark sparkly pink nail polish. Standing outside the corner store with the plastic bags containing licorice candies, Pink Elephant popcorn and Twinkies, Morgan didn't think about either of her sisters, but instead realized Tanya B. was the only person she wanted to share the loot with. They could become friends. More than just babysitter and babysat. And one day, Tanya B. would make sure Morgan become a cheerleader, despite her crooked finger, non-committal lips, and poor coordination.

Tanya B. wasn't home. At practice or something. But Tanya B's mom pressed against the dusty iron door screen, TV blaring in the shadows at her back, stared at Morgan on the doorstep with two plastic bags full of junk food and exhaled her cigarette smoke through the side of her mouth with the jadedness of a TV cop who had seen this sort of thing before.

Her father spanked her severely that night. And then lectured her, on and on, while her mother watched, her arms crossed, vacillating between her stern look and her compassionate face, obviously wanting her father to stop spanking and yelling.

An accidental sob, like a drowning gasp for air. Then another. Then they snowballed until she was almost hyperventilating. Sob after sob. She'd never done this before. Her father stepped back, retreated to the backstage shadows of the kitchen next to her mother. Morgan's fingers clawed into the living room shag rug, a small reptile part of her alert behind the sobs, listening sharply for what would happen next.

"What's that?"

"I think it means she's very sorry," her mother tried.

Her father gave a small nod.

Morgan kept up with sob after sob after sob, until her father eventually fumbled on his boots and clomped down the steps to the garage and her mother turned away from her, withdrew to dicing onions and garlic for the soup, but not before Morgan saw the angry sliver of a headache needle her mother's eyes, blur them to the glare of the kitchen lights. She couldn't hide her concern. It calmed Morgan, that headache.

A break for coffee. Downstairs, Morgan buoys to find Ava sitting in the medical building's café with a cup of tea. She grabs herself a coffee and two cookies, raisin oatmeal, both with cafeteria rigor mortis, and takes them to Ava's table.

"Making it through?"

"Yes, you."

Morgan hands her the cookie.

"Thanks."

"How are your doctors doing?"

"Mostly good. They're very nervous. I can't help but feel for them."

"Yeah," says Morgan taking a crunchy nibble of her cookie, squirreling a glance at Ava's bottom lip. "I know what you mean," she lies. Morgan had gotten all the contemptible future doctors. But Ava's compelling pathos probably made her more compassionate, even loving towards the fumbling med students. Morgan thinks maybe she should try to be more compassionate. More like Ava.

Break over, Ava gives her a little girl wave and thanks her for the cookie. The wave cycles on repeat in Morgan's mind as she shuffles back to her examination room. The invigilator's open office door, his chair empty, lure Morgan to the threshold: four flatscreen monitors thrum in the shadowed room, eskers of tapes of their performances, the doctors' interviews, on the desk in front of the monitors. On the monitor numbered '3', Ava, her face paused, caught in mid-weeping, like Joan of Arc in that old black and white film. Divine. Touched by the hand of God, merely brushed, but then brushed aside. The invigilator must have stepped out to go to the washroom. She can't bear it, the moment architected for her to find the tape. She recons the hallway, realizes the invigilator probably uses bathroom breaks to social media suffer on the toilet like the rest of them, then lunges into the room, hitting eject on the VHS recorder. The TV screen paused on Ava's performance flares a royal blue, incriminating. She slips the VHS tape into her cargo pants pocket and raccoons from the room, willing her walk to a normal pace, wishing the guilt stain blush to pass and hoping no one sees the bulge in her baggy pants. Would be awful to faint from stress just now, surrounded by the worst medical students the school has to offer.

Back in the examination room, the digital clock bullies her with its 11:03 am. She has to wait until she gets home to watch the VHS tape. She momentarily worries the med student on the tape might not pass his or her test without it. But they must have contingencies for such things. The universe must have contingencies for this. She decides she's gone crazy. Or lesbian. Would prefer lesbian. Magazine flips through her women friends in her mind, rehearses kissing each one of them on the mouth or neck, surmises that she really only wants to kiss Ava's mouth, that sad mouth. How would she explain? I want to see you cry. Weep, really. I want to watch you weep. It makes me numb and breathless. The two of them will have this conversation over tea in the café down by the water with the red umbrellas, Ava half-distracted by the rain falling off the awning will make a slow nod at Morgan's words scattering around them like little birds looking for shelter, the burden of such confessions carrying a melancholy familiarity for her. Linoleum-white countenance, impervious, of course she's heard such confessions before. Of course. She will refuse to look at Morgan. Lassitude will prevent her. That and the heat, the humidity clinging to them both. The words sticking to the sweat on the base of her throat like errant strands of hair, the portrait of a woman caught in other people's desires. She might even confess back that she wants Morgan too, but, she will utter a "but," add an impossibility to make the confession parenthetical (engaged, going to war, dying, some melodramatically suitable etc.). Desire arrives predictably too late, futile. Roll credits.

The bell rings, calling them to the next round. 11:10 am. She inhales to better posture in her chair, eyes closed, rallies to endure the sludge of time. She imagines Ava in another room, head at a ponderous angle, the day really just a burdenless burden, her melancholy yet alluring world-weariness.

That night, when Morgan arrives home, the apartment waits hushed. She remembers that Edward has to review a gallery opening and won't be home until later. She slips the VHS tape from her pocket and places it on top of the player in the living room. The invigilator hadn't mentioned the lost tape to anyone. Maybe he didn't want to admit he had lost it. Or maybe the tapes were just backups and one missing tape would go unnoticed.

Morgan opens the fridge door and tries to imagine the sad elements forming a meal. Eggs. Dry pasta in the cupboard. Tabasco. Pickles. Nothing adding up. Decides to just scramble eggs. Edward would have magically produced a meal from the abject cupboards. Edward looks more like her brother than her lover. If Morgan grew a foot taller, mussed herself more unkempt, and grew a little scruff they would forget which one of them was which. A month ago he even came home with the same horned-rimmed glasses as her. She glared at him from the kitchen table, suddenly horny for him but pissed that they would now look like emo twins. Like Wednesday and Pugsley off the Addams Family, a comparison that would delight him, so she didn't make it. She wonders if he, too, would want to watch Ava weep. But she can't bear to share Ava with him. He probably wouldn't. He doesn't understand pain. Or suffering. Which may be precisely why she decided to date him. Like keeping a paint swatch of what happiness and emotional stability looked like in case she was able to someday paint her walls that colour.

Two fried eggs on a plate, tape popped into the player, she sits down on the couch tentative with the remote control, unable to breathe before she presses play. She presses play.

The plate of eggs sits a cold prop on the coffee table. Head in hands, elbows stacked on knees, Morgan is caught, bathed in the blue-tinged light of the VCR footage. Ava's tears, clumsy in their training, now are mere backdrops, upstaged by a consuming pathos, and make Morgan feel her tears are milked from trickery and laziness. Ava speaks all the same words, the same story, the same life as Morgan in her own room, a few walls away. But what Morgan lived with clumsy resentment, an edge of bitter coffee, Ava lived tragically, with ardor. A startling sparkle in her eyes, reminiscent of the vulnerable determination of a Russian heroine striding through snow banks, throwing herself under trains. A melancholy, breathless bottom lip evoking a French heroine, swooning with an opium longing at the railing of an ocean liner tearing her away from Indochina. Morgan would have failed. If Ava had been her fake patient, Morgan would never be able to become a doctor. She would have leapt up, pulled Ava to her feet, held her, forgetting her bruises, her batteredness. She would embrace her and protect her from whatever might come next.

The key in the lock. The door. Edward. She jumps up and ejects the tape like she's been caught having an affair.

"Hey hun," he calls from the hallway.

He asks her questions about her day. She answers sullenly. She's angry at him now, but she can't say why. She feels guilty for being angry with this puppy dog of a man.

Lying in bed, she decides they need relationship counseling. There must be something missing from their relationship that compels her to obsess about Ava's mouth? She scrutinizes him in the cuts of light breaking through the blinds from the street, sleeping jaw slack, angelic little boy softness to his expression on his side of the bed, and she wants to beat him with the pillow or the bedside lamp. But he would wake and ask her what the matter is. And she has no answer. She reminds herself that she chose him. She asked for this.

Her father taught her something about being inarticulate. About secrets. When she was seven, her mother went down south to take care of her mother in the last stages of cancer. Her father standing in front of the fridge with the door open like it might magically cough up another parent to do all the caring or a manual to explain what to do with the three daughters who stood at the threshold to the living room behind him, uncertain how to help. Later, they saw him through the kitchen window watching them play, looking like he just received the news he had children. The mob of kids out front of the trailer thronging like bottle flies in the road and the oldest, Holly, called "Dogpile!" and they all piled on Morgan.

"You're okay," her father said when she came running up the porch to him tear and snot slathered. And then, when her wailing didn't cease, he resorted to distraction: "Look at that bird. I'll bet that's a blue jay," he said then, pointing at a crow. He assumed her desire to correct him would supersede her desire to wallow in tears. He assumed right, the bastard.

"It's a crow," she said, the tears still collecting in the corners of her eyes. She returned to wailing.

"Let me see" he said brusquely reaching for her hand, a tinge of jocularity in his tone, as though it amused him for her to be in such pain, another distraction tactic he had heard his wife use.

She cried out when he grabbed hold of her hand, and then stopped silent when she saw his mouth fall open, his eyes seized wide and fearful. Her finger bent out to the side, the way no finger should ever bend.

In the hospital, the doctor examined her hand while her father, joking stricken from his face, paced in the background.

"How did this happen?" the doctor asked.

"Dogpile."

"What?"

"Dogpile. I jumped in a dogpile."

The doctor, probably his first month in this small town, had only ever heard of the dog pile that comes from a dog's rectum, not the kind made by a pile of children. So he of course had to call a nurse over, as he poorly stifled a smile.

"Alright, Morgan, can you tell the nice nurse how this happened to you?"

"I jumped into a dogpile."

The nurse did a worse job of covering her smile and stifling a snort.

Her father didn't intercede. He wasn't paying attention, just pacing, probably trying to imagine some scenario where he didn't have to tell his wife with the dying mother that their middle child was in the Emergency Ward.

She didn't mean to kick the doctor in the leg. Frustrated with having to explain over and over, and the various health practitioners laughing, she perched on the hospital bed swinging her legs, agitated, when his leg connected with her foot. His face winced, he turned away from her, limped away taking erratic breaths. When he came back moments later he didn't ask about the dogpile anymore. She got orange tiger ice cream on the way home along with the explicit request not to mention the finger on the phone when her mother called. A special secret, her father explained.

Morgan turns from left side to right side that night, hugging her pillow, finally lying facing the ceiling. Edward sleeps like a wood plank. She lies next to him, sleepless and resentful, limbs wrought as tight as mousetrap springs, Ava hanging over her a drowning angel.

The next morning in the café at the university she hunkers over a table trying to slosh a second cup of coffee in before she has to plod upstairs to the scenarios. Then Ava floats above her, emulating Morgan's insomniac visions. Ava with her sack of a purse, her pre-Raphaelite distraction, and faint scent of fruits run rotten, too sweet. She must have lain under the peach tree out back of her house, the dizzy hungry morning bees pressing their insistent fuzzy bodies against her

"Good night?" Morgan asks, cautiously. Ava leans against the table, looking out over the café her eyes unfocused, like her body arrived ten minutes earlier than her soul. She will return. And Morgan longs for this return, finds her lovable even in this sleepwalker form, her clumsy slump in the chair.

"Yes. I think so," she replies, watching the barista bar for her drink.

"I'm ready for this to be over," Morgan lies. She feels the words, their predictability, the script someone has to say on a Thursday to needlessly fill the air. Sure, she hankers for the week to be over, to have a weekend, but it also pains her to think of saying goodbye to Ava. The words hold off that inevitability a little. "I hear next week we are pregnant women who find out they have AIDS."

"Interesting," Ava absently replies as the barista calls out her soy latte and she lurches for the counter to get it. "What are you doing this weekend?" she asks, returning to the table.

"Getting pregnant and AIDS," Morgan jokes. But Ava doesn't look up from her latte, intent on her sip. "Not much," Morgan adds as she suddenly remembers Edward devised a dinner party on Saturday night. He's the king of vegetarian pasta, a title he has given himself and she thinks rather sad and earnest, but she has generously let it stick.

Every relationship finds its equilibrium, she thinks. She remembers how three weeks after her seventeenth birthday, Morgan's mother grew worried that she slept all the time, took her to the family doctor who diagnosed her with mono, the kissing disease, made more embarrassing by the fact that she hadn't yet kissed anyone. Two weeks later she had a boyfriend, Eric, who showed up on her stoop with orange tiger ice cream and ginger ale and every three or four days some new poems he had written, mostly partially digested and regurgitated Depeche Mode lyrics. But sweet. The most attentive man she ever dated.

A month later when the doctor permitted her to return to school, she called Eric, breathless on the yellow phone in the hallway, winding her finger in the coils of the phone cord, inviting him over for what would be, at last, her first kiss. Eric promptly came out to her. Morgan in her mono consumptive state, physically unavailable, created the only circumstances under which Eric would have a girlfriend. Morgan who wanted kisses would not work. She contemplated dating him a little longer, being his alibi. For the ice cream more than the poems. Equilibrium.

Ava looks forlorn, both hands cupped around her beverage like it holds an answer. Morgan sips her drink and then asks, "What are you doing this weekend?"

"Painting my bathroom," Ava says, glancing out at the parking lot, a green car pulling into the last available space. "If I find the right colour paint."

"What colour are you thinking?" How Morgan loves waiting for an answer, so she can study Ava's face, the smooth openness of it, so she can scrutinize it and hope to find some clue to the pathos of her weeping.

"Blue, maybe, but an unexpected blue."

Morgan wonders which came first, the pathos or Ava's mouth. Ava's life seems inanely devoid of drama. Yet, this seems to make her weeping more truthful in Morgan's eyes, like it springs from some unseen authentic core, an existential heaviness, not a soap opera cliché, not the result of someone taking too much pity on themselves and the tragedies they draw around them like throw cushions.

"Time to go," Ava adds, rising from her chair.

Ava gathers up her massive purse, Morgan her courier bag, and they muddle their way to the elevator, Morgan breathless in their silence. She should say more, something that will cloak her reverence. Ridiculous. She trained at two of the best drama schools in the province, was top of her class, walked through praise like rain. And now something as simple as desire hobbles her.

As the elevator doors open, Pete, the director of the Standardized Patient program jogs up behind them, joins them in the elevator.

"Have either of you seen tapes floating around? We lost one yesterday."

"Like a music tape?" asks Ava.

"Exactly. VHS," says Pete. "I thought I had it in the main room, but it's gone missing."

"Nope," says Morgan. She feels nervous, though she knows Pete isn't accusing them. Who would have any reason to steal VHS tapes of student tests after all?

"Oh well," he says, looking down the hallway like the tape might come bouncing towards them. "I guess we'll get started."

Morgan waves a clumsy goodbye to Ava who floats away, waving a hand back above her like a little kite. Where does she get her numinous gestures?

The first med student of the day yawns through the scenario, too exhausted to be anxious. Perfunctory, yet intent. He's got real bed head, not the surfer style kind. Cute, she thinks, imagining waking up beside him, yearning to sleep in, running her fingers through his bed head, longing to covet his pretty eyes without him seeing her looking. Morgan feels too distracted to challenge him. He asks all the relevant questions. He will make a perfectly adequate doctor. Thorough but a little distant. The buzzer complains to mark the end of the scenario.

Morgan stands to leave, then faints. Blackout. She struggles to focus, then sees the ceiling, the green ceiling, then the medical student's confused face. She's never fainted in her life. So when she comes around, the gruff young med student's face hanging over hers, she yells at him, "What did you do?"

Later, he will explain to her how he thought she fainted as part of the scenario. He hadn't noticed the invigilator's panic until he'd already gotten down on the floor and taken her pulse.

Morgan notices the poster on the ceiling of the exam room. A landscape, a beach resort travel poster intended to calm horizontal patients. It latches a corner of her mind, like a sweater thread on a nail. Sickness, white sand, blue water, vacation, the rain falling outside on the Thursday street.

She lurches up on her elbows.

"Take it easy, slow even breaths." The med student intent, holds her hand in his thick paw. He is different now. She sits up, wrapping her arms around her knees for stability, his burnt umber eyes, pressing, searching her face. He cares. And she begins to sob. Her sadness has nothing of Ava's composed melancholia. Morgan's cheeks soaked with tears, she chokes surprised, her mouth gasping, snot running from her nose, chest heaving for breaths.

And then that burnt-umber-eyed med student lunges in, his arms encircling her, crushing her fiercely to his shirt, his chest muscles warm on her cheek through the fabric. She thinks to push away, the shock of it, but then she inhales and he smells spicy, like the kind of cologne a grandmother buys in a drugstore and gives her grandson. Something so sincere in the heat of his chest, the pulse of his heart, the manly cologne. Held by cliché. She clings to it. Her fingers press into the muscles flanking his back, the thick muscled chest presses warm against her through his dress shirt.

"Kevin," says the invigilator a little sternly. Then this man named Kevin pulls away and she quickly lets her hands drop, pretending he held her, not the other way around.

"It's okay," she says as the invigilator hands her Kleenex and she takes it, rubbing her nose. Ava and Pete crowd the doorway, eyes wide with worry. Of course. Break time between scenarios. A dimple of concern in Ava's forehead. Morgan's weeping was wracked and rude, clumsy without grace. "Pete, I think maybe I need to go home."

Pete nods. "Absolutely," he says still nodding. "Should I call Edward?" he asks.

Morgan shakes her head, blushes slightly, steals a furtive look to see if Ava registered that she has a man named Edward in her life. She inhales shakily, and half shudders out a sigh, shakes off the tears. The beach poster on the ceiling calls to her, cerulean waves insisting peacefulness. Ava's still standing in the doorway. Morgan grimaces a smile, wanting her to leave, not witness anymore of this wreckage. Ava mirrors the small smile, but her whole face needs to work to provide the reassurance, to overcome her melancholy mouth. She doesn't seem surprised, but of course, these kinds of small disasters must dot the landscape of her life. Then Ava holds out her hand to Morgan, like the broken woman on the floor has passed some test, crossed a threshold into the land of the weary and the tragic. So Morgan takes her hand, rises gangly, steps into her embrace, their chins resting on each other's shoulders. Then they part, covers of a book, and like cathedral novices glide down the hallway holding hands, sisters of the downturned mouth, waiting for a good doctor.

# CHIAROSCURO

*"Certainly it is very difficult to be certain just
how completely one is frightened in being living.
Certainly it is very difficult to be really certain
just how much one is not frightened in being
one being living."*

— "MI-CAREME," GERTRUDE STEIN

# CHIAROSCURO

**ABEL LOVES SLEEP**, so that camping trip with his brother might have ruined it for him. His brother Dwayne, rhymes with Cain, his mother thought that was funny, growled at him as he tripped out of the tent and stumbled to the fire the first morning.

Ignoring the growl, Abel focused on survival. "You made coffee?"

"None for effing you." Dwayne had compromised on cursing since he had kids.

"Why's that?"

"You bloody kept me up all night. Like a badger trying to fuck a pig." The curse compromise failed, often. "Errrrgk, weeeeee, errrrgk, weeeee," he imitated, complete with the frustrated badger and alarmed pig faces.

Single for half a decade now, snoring was a new development for Abel. Not much for sleepovers either, he had no opportunity to assault anyone with his snores. Until the camping trip. Dwayne's idea of a birthday gift: "You're gonna get the cancer on that computer all the time in that hamster home you shit in."

His brother poked the fire's embers into catching the new wood, like they'd done him wrong too, a cup of black camp coffee clutched to his chest, the sleeplessness crusty in the corner of his eyes. Abel considers himself a discreet man, concerned with wearing too much cologne so he wears none, worried about sitting in a seat meant for the elderly, a man who can't enjoy movies or plays if he feels he's blocking someone else's view. He's six foot three inches, so he watches most movies on DVD. Snoring.

Abel dreaded it when the barber held up that little hand

mirror after the haircut, tried to show him the back of his head. He had trusted until now that the things out of his sight, his purview, were beyond his control. So he'd rather not be reminded of them. Yet this new unconscious habit plagued his thoughts, a dark side of the moon kind of question. Schrödinger's cat. Or dog? No, Pavlov had the dog. He could have been perfectly content not knowing about the snoring, but now he knew: a flaw that could very realistically keep him single if he did ever meet someone who might want to sleep over.

Sunday afternoon, Dwayne drops Abel off in the parking lot of his building, glances up at the building through the truck windshield with disdain. They've had this conversation before: for Dwayne, apartment living is for drifters, unmarried women, and people missing spines. Abel lets the look slide, thanks his brother, closes the door to the cab and grabs his duffel bag from the back of the truck. He loves his little six-storey character building, defiant in among the looming grey-glass towers flanking it on all sides.

Later, unpacking his pack at the front door, the spicy, burnt-wood campfire smell exhaling in the room, he puzzles out what to do about his snoring problem. His brother could be exaggerating. The camp smell threatens to contaminate the living room so he strips down to nothing, throws every article of clothing into the washing machine, and closes himself in the shower to scrub the outdoors off.

Dried, fresh boxers and socks on, he slides to his home office desk and Googles "sleep disorders," overstating the issue. In Iceland a five-year-old girl sleepwalked in her underwear and a toque five miles to the next town; a man in Colorado camping with friends stumbled out of his tent in his underwear, past his friends who were telling ghost stories, and walked off the edge of a cliff while they watched; a man in Bath would grip his wife like a life preserver, weeping, bruising her arms while he slept. Snoring might be the least of it.

Proof. He needs proof. He digs around in his desk drawer and finds his digicam. It can record up to six hours at a time. He could tape himself sleeping. He could investigate his own snoring. A small part of his brain wonders what the hell he will do with that info, but the rest of his brain has a plan. He will tape himself the next Friday night. He doesn't have to be up Saturday morning, just in case he has a hard time falling asleep under the pervy gaze of the camera. He tells himself he will be the only one to see the footage. And he promises himself he'll delete it when he's done, keep it a secret. Like he never looked in the hand mirror.

Sleep fascinates Abel. What he can control about it, he has: hypo-allergenic covers on the pillows and mattress, silk-filled duvet to regulate temperature and reject dust mites, over 400 thread count Egyptian cotton sheets, changed weekly and replaced every six months from a bedding supplier in Boston. Blackout curtains and a humidifier to compensate for the electric heat. No caffeine after 3:00 pm and he exercises daily, walking on the treadmill in his home office. He tracks each night's rest, duration, and REM sleep registered on an app on his smartphone based on his sleep movements. Abel more than anyone should be able to ensure a consistently excellent sleep. Yet in the last month his sleep patterns have been unpredictable, a night of great sleep followed by three terrible nights and then another inexplicable good night. The possibility of getting more data on the sleep issue galvanizes his snore research plan.

Friday night, he sets the camera on the dresser under his flatscreen TV, a random poetry anthology his mother found at a garage sale under the back end of the camera to tilt it at the angle necessary to frame his pillow in the shot. Finally a use for poetry. He finds himself pacing a little while he brushes his teeth, outside his windows little boxed lives glitter, stacked up to the sky. Checks his email a couple more times than usual before bed. No red light so he knows the camera is not recording, but still he feels like it's watching.

When he finally hits the red *rec* button and lies down, his first thought is that he might not sleep at all. But, then, a massive, deep sleep. He doesn't wake even once, not even to pee in the middle of the night. When he finally strains through sandy eyes to see the clock on the bedside table, 9:06 glares back angry red at him, but the camera's red light is off. He slept for more than eight hours, a dreamless, pure sleep, despite his self-consciousness the night before. Sleep has been erratic lately, he notes again, looking at his smartphone app: nights of drunk, full-throated REM followed by nights in the shallows, constant flipping and itchy feet.

Abel leaves the camera where it is, lording over him its sleep secrets, postpones checking it out. He opts for a bowl of muesli and yogurt, a cup of coffee, opening some old mail, then he definitely needs a second cup of coffee to properly wake up. Instant-message windows proliferate as his coworkers get to work. He works on the programming side of a company that designs user interfaces, which means his work borders on invisible to the designers so he can work from home. Suits him not to have to interface with the users, he joked once to Dwayne, who stared at him blankly.

Abel decides to upload the footage to the computer first so he can manipulate it with the software. And the sound, any potential snores, might be more discernable. He passes the cursor over 'upload,' stares at it but then realizes he can't wait any longer. He snaps up the camera, flips open the side screen, and presses the menu button, his curiosity smothering his anxiety.

He decides it would make the most sense to click on the middle of the six hours, like cutting a biopsy. Certainly, if he snores, he probably doesn't get into the thick of it until the middle of deep sleep. In the absence of a degree in sleep, he forges his own somnolent logic.

He hits the mid point on the time code. On the blue blankets, in low light, a sleeping man. He holds his breath while he watches himself sleep. Can't help it. He sleeps on his side, holding a pillow in his arms with a grip no living creature could survive. No revelation here. Once when he had to stay in the hospital overnight he'd woken to a nurse watching him, watching how he held the pillow. She'd started when he caught her, bolted back to the nurses' station.

He selects the zoom function on the screen, scrutinizes the open-mouthed face, the mussed hair. He feels, for the briefest moment, the desire to run his fingers through his own hair, sort it out. As children, his brother used to make fun of him for combing his hair right before bed. Silly, for sure. Who would see him sleeping with well-groomed hair? Still, seeing himself on the screen, he wants to get his comb.

A little snoring. More heavy breathing, really. Nothing to warrant his brother's badger and pig impersonations over the campfire coffee. Maybe his brother has sleep apnea or having kids has made him a light sleeper. Abel's sleeping self turns over to his right side. Since when does he sleep on his right side? As far as Abel knew, he could only ever sleep on his left. He even claimed so in his last relationship, argued he had to sleep on the right side of the bed, so he could sleep on his left side facing away from Julie. He believed people should sleep this way, like book ends )(, not parentheticals ( ). And he assumed the rest of the world would find some way to be the proper left to his right. Julie saw things differently: )) or (( all she could imagine. So they parted.

)                                                        (.

The snoring is comparable on his unexpected right side, so he clicks the mouse to an hour earlier on the time code. Sleep noise rasps a little louder there. In this pose, he slept at a quarter turn, half facing the ceiling. Back sleepers snore more. He'd heard that somewhere. Was he a secret back sleeper? He used to think he could only sleep left; he squints at this alien man slumbering in his bed, wondering what other secrets he withholds. He clicks to the four-hour point on the footage. He sleeps back on his left side.

Something slides in front of the camera. Someone. Blocks the perspective.

Abel cries out, almost drops the camera as he jumps in his seat.

He backs up the tape a few seconds. Watches the dark figure flare past and obscure the lens again. The figure unidentifiably close, obscuring the room. Someone trespassed his room while he slept. He quickly looks around the room. Is anything missing? Was he robbed in his sleep? The footage continues to play. On the camera screen movement flashes again. At the edge of the bed. On the left side to his right. A woman. Shoulder-length black hair, a pale, long face and neck. She pauses at the edge of the bed. He can't see her expression from the camera's perspective. She stands right against the edge of the bed, her knees pressed into the mattress. Is she taking off her shoes? Is she watching him sleep?

He doesn't know her. Only two people have keys to the apartment, his mother and Dwayne, who has a key in case something terrible happens. Neurotic emergency buddies. Maybe the caretaker of the condo building. He might have a key. But the caretaker's a single man. So how did this woman get in? Oh, and the cleaning lady has a key. But she doesn't look anything like the cleaning lady. Couldn't even be a relative. Did he have the locks changed when he moved in? Yes, he would predictably obsess about that.

She lowers herself to the bed in slow motion, extending her

legs and laying herself down beside him. She didn't get the book ends memo. She lies parenthetical to him ((. What is it with these people, he thinks to himself, then laughs a stuttered laugh, as though her sleeping position is the most objectionable thing about her climbing into bed with him. She faces his sleeping back. What does she see?

From the camera's angled perspective, she looks like she's following him, sleepily shadowing him on a horizontal plane. He uploads the video to the computer so he can examine her image more closely.

Four hours, ten minutes. He presses fast forward. Her still form, still as his shadow, breaths like eyelash flutters.

Four hours, forty minutes, he turns over and faces her, sleeping on his right side again, full parenthetical to her ( ). All wrong. He's never slept this way with anyone. Said goodnight maybe, a little kiss, then turned away. A decent person would turn away. At least )). She doesn't. He presses play, returning the clip to normal speed. He's snoring, with moments of crescendo, as though to clear an obstruction with forced air. But still she doesn't move. So close. And, absurdly, he now smiles in his sleep, like he takes pleasure in this wrong sleeping arrangement.

Five hours, forty minutes. She rises from the bed and slips on her sandals. She turns back to him and he wonders if she will kiss him. He's watching his life like it's a TV show. And this is what he wants to have happen next, for her to kiss him, gently, goodnight. But she skirts the bed, past the camera, blocking the lens again. Then gone.

He leans back from the computer screen. He clicks the clip back an hour on the time code and pauses the image. )). He shuffles to the kitchen, a habitual action of bread slice, butter, cheese slice, bread slice, butter, his mind scanning over the mental footage of the girl in his bed, and then only the burnt butter smell jarring his mind to recognize he made a grilled cheese sandwich and it might be burning.

Chewing his sandwich, staring out at the towering people-nesting colonies watching all their flatscreen TVs, he realizes he will have to go to sleep again tonight. What if she comes back? Should he call the police? Should he stay awake and confront her? He searches the apartment looking for signs of forced entry, scratches around the lock on the door, windows she might have climbed in, also to see if she might have stolen anything valuable, but all his comics and collector cards remain nestled in their plastic sheaths in the cabinet drawers. Nothing.

He'll set the camera to tape tonight as well. He uploaded the footage of the previous night to his computer, so he won't lose the evidence. She didn't steal anything. She didn't do anything to him while he slept, except sleep in the wrong position. Well, technically, she slept in one wrong position and he followed it up with another. But he didn't know she slept beside him. She should have been the responsible sleeper.

He showers and shaves before bed that night, even gargles mouthwash. And he combs his hair. He wonders if he's always unconsciously combed his hair before bed because of this, an awareness he might be sleep-visited. He gives the apartment a quick once-over tidy. He can't remember the last time he had a guest over. Dwayne refuses to be this far off the ground in an earthquake zone. "If you don't fall to your death or get crushed by this asbestos trap, you'll get cut to bits by the glass from all those shit towers on all sides. All that glass has gotta go somewhere."

Abel positions the camera in the same place under the flat-screen, the poetry book under the back to tilt it at the right angle. Then he lies down, cheek to pillow. He fears he won't fall asleep. Feels like Christmas Eve. Maybe, like Santa, she won't come if he doesn't sleep. Turns to his right side to see if he can fall asleep that way, the wall, the stack of books on the shelf, the sounds of traffic outside, all more compelling than sleep. Turns to his left side and, a small flood of images, darting fishes, then the sea floor falls away.

An awful sleep. In the morning, rain slicks the bedroom window, umbrella traffic on the wet concrete below. When he plays the footage the left side of the bed prairies flat. He scans the whole six hours, but nothing, just hours and hours of him snoring and drooling and kicking like a dog. He slumps back, a half-eaten bowl of cereal sogging in front of him, wonders if maybe she won't return. Maybe she visited by accident. Perhaps she serially sleeps, a different bed each night. Maybe she cares about the environment, reducing the number of beds tossed in landfills each year. Or she skulks about, some kind of mythic creature that finds sustenance in the breath of the lonely.

That night, he combs his hair, but doesn't shave, starts the camera, and lies down. An idea. He pops up and switches the camera off. He writes a note, two sentences, ponders, then adds a third. Places it on her side of the bed. Then presses the red button on the camera and lies back down. His thoughts slur into sleep with a little hope and a little despair.

The note says, "My name is Abel. I prefer bookends to parentheticals. Please stay."

An awful sleep, persistent chasing dreams, precipices, a moment of flight and then falling, then running, the loop swallowing itself. On the footage in the morning, she returns. She cuts in front of the camera, she leans against the bed, and she picks up the note. She reads it. Then she places it back just where she found it and exits the camera frame. Without lying down.

Abel slumps back in the desk chair, shoulders hitching up.

He forgets to eat lunch, ignores the blossoming instant-message windows as his coworkers reach out across the ether to him, blinds closed, blanket and pillow on the couch, haze of channels, empty Cantonese delivery containers piling up on the glass coffee table. The world feels askew.

He tapes his sleep for the next four nights, awful sleeps, but she does not return.

Sleep, thin and dreamless, diminishes into a sad thing.

Then a week later, he comes up with a plan. She must have a key. Which means she must have keys, and this means she probably only practices her nocturnal visitations in the same general locale. This apartment building. That night he camps out in the hallway at the end of his floor. Most of the tenants skew geriatric or professional enough they rise with the sun and collapse soon after sunset, particularly on a Wednesday night, so he sets up camp at 11:30, armed with a thermos of coffee, throw pillows from the couch, and a blanket. The plan could work, so long as he stays awake. He has to stay vigilant. Once she's discovered, he knows she'll never come back.

He's brought a book. Something about dreams, which he sees now wasn't the wisest choice, so he gulps his way through the thermos of coffee before 1:00 am. Around 2:30 am, his bladder almost forcing him to abandon his post, he hears footsteps on the stairs. He feels vulnerable on the floor, pulse shuddering his chest and neck. Will the steps stop on his floor? A tenant coming home will demand that Abel explain why he's sitting in the hallway with a blanket and couch pillows reading a book. He could say he locked himself out. The steps scuff closer, and they slow, as though the stepper nears his or her floor. The door opens. She scans his face, one eyebrow pulling down in confusion.

She lets out a little scream, flails for the door behind her.

"Wait!" he calls. "I promise, I just want to talk. Just talk."

She freezes, like in a kid's game, doesn't turn around.

The large ring of keys in her left hand, her boots that look like slippers, her grey, comfy sweatpants.

"Well?" she says, glancing over her shoulder.

"Oh," he said. "I didn't think you'd stop."

She rolls her eyes and rocks back on the balls of her feet, swivels to —

"It's just, I was hoping you'd come back. Come back and sleep at my place. Sometime."

She seems paralyzed by his proposal, the bare desperation of it.

"I sleep better with you. I just mean sleep. I promise I won't leave any more notes. I have a great bed. Do you remember? I have the best sheets. Hypo-allergenic duvet. My mother taught me that. Only the best sheets. So you could come back. And you don't need to worry. Just sleep."

Her shoulders drop a subtle inch, a small jangle from the keys, she hovers with the dust motes.

He thinks she might have nodded.

"I do like how you snore," she says. The stairwell door sinks closed as her footsteps thud down the stairwell.

He tried.

He picks up the book and pillow and blanket and shuffles back to his apartment. In the bathroom he brushes his teeth and brushes his hair. In a small moment of hopefulness he sets the camera on the poetry book under the TV. Then he lies down, 1:23 am, and sleeps the five and a half hours he has until the alarm. A thick, quenching sleep.

The next morning, the sun glaring through the gaps between the towers outside, he scans the footage as he chews buttered toast before work, a little less hopeful. But 2:34 am, she wanders into the camera frame. Same side of the bed. She glances over her shoulder in the direction of the camera, pins its gaze in hers. She strides up to the lens, blocks the light, and then the recording ends.

# MIRRORBALL

# MIRRORBALL

**BEN USED TO CALL ME** only late at night, blurry drunk, too drunk to go home but not so drunk that he couldn't operate a phone if he had one eye closed and said the number over and over. I don't know how he managed to always remember my number. It was, after all, my number, not our number, not the number we had when we were together. It was the number I got after we both left the old one behind to curse someone else. But I joke. Now he just emails me, seems cautious around what his therapist called boundaries, a hesitancy in his missives, like a bleated-out bovine cowering next to a familiar electric fence.

So he emails me. "Dear Nick." Hears we're in the same city. I'm back for a few months. Someone saw me. Says he has something to tell me. "To show you, actually," he adds in case he's not being cryptic enough. I email back, ask where and when. He responds before I can close the email program: "Café at the corner of Davie and Denman. Tomorrow morning. 11:00." It's not really like him to be this specific. See, he's the guy who perennially sets off on road trips, errands or to housewarming parties without an address, without directions, without a compass or an umbrella. He calls this optimistic.

For the last few years we've only seen each other in other cities. A martini or two on Bloor in Toronto, pancakes at a café in Studio City, California, and one time half an ice cream each in Santa Monica, halved by a collision with a scantily clad rollerblader. We're rarely in this city at the same time. That and the conversations we've had to have since things ended nine and a bit years ago have come sporadically, carefully, with sometimes surprisingly persistent wounds and little eye contact.

The last time, the ice cream collision, had been a gush, a rupture. Ben had tripped over scar tissue and decided to be done with it. Reconstituting our history then, icecreamless, meant offering each other histories we could barely remember except as a slide show of smudged colours and hurts. We snipped the last of the stitches; this, we both felt, was at last the letting go. So this email, this call for a coffee at a specific café with a specific address, perplexes me.

And then I forget about the coffee date until the next morning, Saturday, when I wake late, around nine to my cell spasming to a text from him: "10:45?" So I text back "k" and rush for the shower. Coffees with exes require almost the same prep as first dates, all with the same demand: desire me above all others. Or at least pretend.

I shower fast, face scrub some colour into my cheeks, dry my hair thoroughly so it won't hang limp, won't reveal its fading thickness. I am out the door, down the street, five minutes late, and can see his knees bouncing under the café table from half a block away.

He's chewing the inside of his cheek as I hug him hello so that his mouth seems slightly askew. The mouth chewing I don't miss, the askew smile taunts with lovely.

He's bought us both drinks already. Me an Americano. And him a latte.

"Thanks," I take a sip. "Alright, so what's the big surprise?"

"Not yet." He is quaking with the desire to reveal this secret and still he waits. Not at all like him. He is the kind of man who buys gifts at the last minute so he has less time to be tortured with the secret of what he bought. I try to remind myself that I don't necessarily know him anymore. A threshold between not knowing him and knowing him better than anyone. Lost and familiar.

We talk about the weather a little, his job, how it's new, how it's half soul-stealing, half free Post-its. He keeps looking out the window as he answers, perpetually distracted.

Then he sits up with a lurch, points through the wall of glass towards the bay, towards the grey water pressing there, the freighters standoffish. "There," he adds, and I follow his fingers specifically. To a couple. A tall guy, blond with broad shoulders, and a shorter guy, pale skin, black hair.

"Cute," I reply, sipping the Americano, wishing he had ordered it for here and saved the paper and plastic.

"Don't you see?"

"The couple?"

"Yes, the couple."

"Yeah, they're sweet."

"You don't see."

I lean back in my chair, then lean forward scrutinizing them once more. "I have no idea what you're talking about."

"They're us."

I was about to take a drink of my Americano, and now the cup hangs halfway to my mouth, hangs in the air, my brain momentarily stalled.

"They're us ten years ago."

"You mean like in a Star Trek wormhole through time way or in a close resemblance way?"

"They're us."

"And, hold on, how did you know they were going to be here right now?"

"I didn't really. But I see them every Saturday morning. They get drinks, go for a walk and talk about how their relationship is ending."

That sounded more than familiar. We had joked about how we might have to buy one of the benches by the lagoon because we used it too much, the one near the footbridge and the rocks where the turtles beached and sunned themselves. It was our bench in the last days, the words etched into it all measurements of the time we'd been there, though none of them carved by us, but by strangers who snuck in while we slept, dreaming of other words to say tomorrow, to stave off the end.

"Wait, how do you know?"

"Know what?"

"What they talk about? The relationship. That it's ending."

He looks like he's stalling, looks out over the water.

"You followed them?"

"Only once or twice. Come on, it's too amazing not to."

"Alright, I see a little similarity, but I think this . . . I hate to say this, but I think this says more about what you're going through than some miracle of time and space."

"Fuck, alright," he stands up then. "Come with me. I'll prove it to you."

"I'm not going to stalk them."

"I'll stalk them then. You just have to follow."

"Have you talked to your therapist about this?"

We stalk them. They walk along the seawall, and we walk along the path just above. We can't hear what they say, can only read their body language. They do not hold hands. There are no overt displays of emotion. They seem to be on a perfectly average walk except that neither of them smile and both seem inordinately interested in either the trees, the water, or the sky — clearly relationship trouble. And it's a little clearer to me as we follow that they do look disturbingly like us, but, uncannily, slightly different, as though variations on a theme: the tall one, blond like me, has eyes that are more recessed, smaller ears; the short one has red cheeks to Ben's pale

ones and his cranium doesn't seem so round. But to list these differences seems ludicrous, like trying to deny family resemblance.

The path we're walking on rises up from the water and the
trees between our path and the seawall thicken and multiply
until they obscure the view. I quicken my pace, hoping to get
ahead of them by the time the paths meet up on the other side
of the trees so at least we can look a little less conspicuous.

"You see it," Ben says.

"I don't know what I see," I say. "And I think this is going to
end badly."

"Maybe they're our doppelgangers."

"Yeah. What does that mean?"

"Think the theory is that if you meet your doppelganger you
both explode or something."

"But I have a date tonight."

"You do? With who?"

We crest the hill, look down towards the Second Beach pool,
the picnic area, but can't see the seawall directly below us for
the trees. I hope we haven't lost them.

"No one you know."

"What's he like?"

"Total bastard. I can't date another nice guy. It would kill me."

Ben says nothing. I tilt my head, pretending to look up at the
road by the putting range. His face is blank, unreadable. Unreadable feels like vertigo after you've stopped dating someone. But
the trade off, it seems, is that there are fewer days when I am
leashed to what every throat-clearing cough and foot shuffle
might mean, the weight of knowing Ben's own personal language
more than my own. The claustrophobia of care.

We need not worry about losing them: they took the sea wall
and we took the vista-less only other, thus more Frostian, path —
limited options.

When we reach the outdoor pool railing and turn to walk where the sea wall skirts it, I throw a look over my shoulder and see they've turned the opposite direction onto the path that leads towards the lagoon.

I see it long before it happens. And I look at Ben for a moment and realize he knows and is waiting for me to realize: they're headed towards our bench.

"Really?"

"Well, last time yeah. Don't know if they're headed there this time." Ben turns back and follows them.

"Seriously? There have to be some sixty park benches in the park."

"343. I looked it up," he calls back over his shoulder.

"And they're breaking up on our bench?" I start after Ben.

Ben turns and walks backwards as I catch up to him. "Looks like it's not ours anymore."

They're pretty far ahead of us so that when we get to the footbridge we can see they are already sitting on the bench looking north over a hidden pocket of the lagoon. We stop on the crest of the footbridge looking south, cast a couple of casual glances in their direction.

"Well, we can't hear shit from here," he says, perturbed with my subpar sleuthing skills.

"You want to go sit beside them on the bench?"

"Funny guy. Last Saturday I was able to stand behind those raspberry bushes behind them. I could catch some of what they said."

"Alright. Don't you think we'll look weird just standing there by the road?"

"It's Stanley Park. We'll just be two more weirdos."

"Comforting."

We quietly station ourselves on the other side of the raspberry bushes.

I can't hear anything the me one says. He mumbles, face hangs lapwards. I can hear the Ben one though. He says he doesn't understand either. Something about maybe not being a relationship kind of guy. Or that he doesn't want to be in a relationship. His words are a little rushed, like he's afraid of what he's saying. He shakes his head and looks up across the pond. Then leans back, slides his arm lightly behind the me one but not touching, garlanding him along the back of the bench. Close but not quite. I remember those days. Where touching Ben seemed impossible, the air marble between us. And still so unbearably close, those last three weeks. We were broken up but still living together, trying to fit two halves of a broken planet into a small one-bedroom apartment.

How other people can become habits. He cooks the dinner, I wash the dishes and complain about how he uses every dish in the kitchen to make one simple meal. I leave my underwear on the bathroom floor and leave the shower curtain unstuck from the tiles so shower water leaks out and he dries up the puddles and throws the towel and my underwear in the dirty laundry with a huff and a bang of the hamper lid, insulted by cotton briefs and water. Even now, so many years later, my breath latches to my ribs thinking of all this accounting. Like telling someone a dream the next morning, how it morphs and becomes so plainly and crushingly literal. Love made us too literal.

"He wants to see other people," whispers Ben.

It's like I'm hearing him explain our breakup to a third party. My brain momentarily stopped by the sledgehammer of my pulse.

He wants to see other people.

I look towards the two men on the bench. Realize it's the other Ben talking, not the other me. The words I once said to Ben are now said by this Ben to this other me. All the similarities that were falling into place fall all out onto the gravel like jigsaw pieces.

And it's embarrassing that in that moment I notice the nape of that other Ben's neck, smooth and recently cleaned up by some barber. He is clean cut. The other me looks unkempt, slept in. How one of them is making himself beautiful for other people while the other chews sleep and tries to hide behind the dust motes.

I long to see this other Ben's face, to look into his eyes, cold lake water, see how he's already in among the limbs of headless bodies sloughing and brushing off all that other me's finger-prints, smells, dirtying him clean. I move a little to the left, trying to see him better. A stone gives way. I grab the blackberry bush for balance but puncture my palm with thorns. I gasp a small yelp, catch Ben's glare.

We both notice the silence at the same time. The two men are no longer talking. We turn towards the bench. They both look directly at us, the two older versions of them hiding behind the blackberry bushes eavesdropping.

Ben looks at me, then looks at them.

I step forward, round the bush with my hand extended to first past Ben and then to past me. "I'm Nick." They shake my hand, a little bewildered. "This is Ben," I say gesturing back at him. I glance in his direction and see how we must have looked, perverts behind the bush.

"We're sorry to intrude."

Ben takes a step forward. "It's just that you guys seem so —"

"We're really sorry," I try to get Ben to look at me, to signal him somehow. It's bad enough that we look like perverts. I don't want to look like insane time-travel perverts to these two. "We'll leave you to your privacy." I nod and hold my hand out as though to calm nervous critters, then walk back towards the footbridge. Ben still stands, not wanting to relinquish whatever brought him to follow them. "Ben."

He looks at me, then lowers his head a little and catches up to me. I give a little wave to the past versions of us still standing beside the park bench, still either baffled or astonished, and we walk to the footbridge.

On the crest of the bridge, I stop and look out across the creek towards Second Beach. We're far enough away from the couple that we won't seem like we're creeping them anymore. Ben stops to my right, then leans in on the concrete railing with me. "Maybe they would have understood," he tries.

"Understood what exactly? Two older men nostalgically perving out on the destruction of their relationship?"

"That's not . . ." Ben slumps onto the railing a little more. "It's more complicated than that."

We both look out over the creek, the ocean in the distance, the edge of the meadow where the waddling ducks search the underbrush. Below us a raccoon washes his black plastic fork claws in the creek water. He's not supposed to be out during the day; maybe he's rabid.

"I don't know what I wanted," says Ben.

"I know. Was hard to turn away from." I push back from the concrete railing. "I should head home. Date tonight."

"Yeah, you said."

"Excuse me," says a voice from behind us.

The couple has caught up to us.

"Hi," says young Ben. "I'm Bryan." And he holds his hand out to shake mine. "This is Neil," he says gesturing to young me beside him. Young me blushes, says nothing. Most peculiar.

They agree this is Twilight Zoney and that they see the resemblance too. We all exchange phone numbers, and I have a small vertigo, like we are spinning a roulette wheel. With all those numbers, almost anything could happen next.

And, as with most things, vast possibility turns out to be pointless as things go just as they should. Young Ben calls me the next morning, too eager to wait even one more day. Of course he calls about half an hour after I call young me, curious about that blush, that familiar yet alien blush. How can he blush when I haven't blushed since the schoolyard.

Young Ben asks if I am busy on Friday night, wants to do something. Says he will make all the arrangements. Most peculiar. So I say sure, curious to see what will happen next. Ben has never made all the arrangements. Ben mostly weighs options until he's forced to choose or someone chooses for him. I submit to young Ben, with trepidation like I am agreeing to go along with a trick.

On the phone, half an hour earlier, young me sounded breathless and too amenable. I suggested we grab coffee beverages and go for a walk. He paused. I asked what was it. He asked if we could do anything in the world but get coffee beverages and walk and added that for him walking with coffee beverages meant the end of things now.

"That makes sense," I replied.

I don't want to tell any of this to Ben. Partly because I subtly criticized him for having too overt an interest in this couple, these two men falling out of love. But mostly because I suspect that I got phone calls and he didn't. He's beautiful, Ben, but his beauty is something that sneaks up on you. I mean, he's cute to start, but not bowl-you-over cute. The bowl-you-over part comes later, the kind where you're bowled before you know it. And I sometimes fear I am the opposite. That I bowl you over then underwelm you later. But it usually meant I got phone calls. I remember Ben told me once that he felt we had a lot in common, but that the most significant thing was that we both found me hot. Unkind, yes, but not untrue.

And these things too, are true. Late Wednesday night, leaning over a younger me, shirtless, juice-blush stain spreading
down his neck, I have to admit I have often fantasized about this.
Though I was never older in those fantasies. And there was no
blushing to be had. But as I lean on one arm and struggle to undo
his belt buckle, that blush wildfire up his neck, his hands shaking
on my belt buckle, his head lolling like cattle in the paddock, I
realize it is nothing like I imagined. What I had always longed
for was to adore myself the way others adored me, to see at last
what they saw. Here, hand reaching down into this younger me's
underwear, I realize this isn't me at all. And instead of finding
myself in his image, everything he does makes me feel older,
more frail, dry as wood rot, thin as last leaves on the tree. I play
a part, leaning down on him, pressing myself against him, being
the man who can make him blush, not the man I am. Maybe the
man I was. And as his head tilts back, throat bulged forward, the
blush surging across his chest, I play the part.

And this, too, is true. Young Ben organizes an extraordinary
first date. Dinner at a sushi place I have never been to down in
Yaletown, tickets to a French film I've never seen at the Festival
theatre, and he insists on picking me up. And if I was worried
that I would feel too much like it used to be between Ben and I,
too much of an image of what we once were, this new Ben will
have nothing to do with it. Later that night, young Ben hanging
over me, fumbling with my belt buckle, his broad chest looming
over my face, I wonder if I could blush if I even wanted to. And
then I wonder if this younger Ben knows I was with the younger
me just two nights ago. And then I wonder who I am in amongst
their limbs, their longing, their mottled grief.

Young Ben undoes my belt buckle, I lean in and nuzzle my
head into his chest. He pushes me back, his chin driving down to
his chest, tensed and gripped to his own pleasure. I am nowhere

nearby. I've never seen a Ben like this. This Ben is a man caught in sensation, no interest in what is going on with me or who might be looking through the bedroom window (which, incidentally, is wide open), or what I might think of this particular contortion or spasm. Combustible. A sheen of sweat on his shoulders, chest, washes the air. I want to behold him; I keep forgetting to have sex. The streetlight through the blinds washes around him, hung above me. Then, a furtive thrust, he lunges down and his mouth is on my neck, his hands reach round me, and I am vice gripped, but he leans back, hips thrusting, head thrown back, gone again, and no way to follow.

He sleeps, his back to me, though he holds onto my hand, holds me to his back. I'd normally leave, think a date is over after all these naked contortions. But that move is predicated on knowing what comes next. And this Ben, this visceral tango of a Ben, leaves me cheek to the nape of his neck listening to the ellipses of his breath.

Still, somewhere around 3:00 am his hand lets mine go. He is deep into a slack-jawed sleep. The smooth skin along his cheek. The base of his throat with its small insistent pulse. I remember a painting of a naked shepherd sleeping, muscular in repose, a faery beholding him. At a certain point I stopped imagining I sleep like that. At a certain age sleep becomes corporeal and its own kind of hideousness. I can't sleep fearing he might wake up and see me unconscious and drooly and snoring. And morning light will be unkind. It's time to go. Leave something of me a mystery.

**THE NEXT MORNING**, Saturday, I meet old Ben for coffee, same place, same time.

"You're not considering following them again are you?" I ask sitting down, an Americano already in front of me.

His mouth moves a little sideways, a small shake of his head, tolerating me. "I have something to tell you."

"First show me, now tell me. These little get-togethers are starting to make me nervous."

He looks down at his hand holding his latte, then looks out at the water. "I've been on dates with those guys."

I take a sip of my Americano, a little taken aback. "Both of them?"

"Yes. I was only sort of interested in the blond one —"

"The me."

"The younger you."

"Ouch."

"But then the other one called me too."

"They both called you?"

"Yeah. The next day," he looks down at his hands in front of him. "I was going to call and tell you right away, but then I couldn't figure out why I felt I should tell you. And I wondered if they had called you too. And then I wanted to know, but I didn't want to know."

"So you went out with them?"

"Yes, one on Tuesday and one on Wednesday. Blond one on Tuesday."

I want to say right there that I went out with them too, but I can't find a way to say it that doesn't sound competitive. I guess I didn't realize I felt competitive until right then. They called him first. He'd been with them first. As Ben talks, as he explains how he felt when they called him, how he felt guilty for not calling and telling me immediately, I find myself scrutinizing his face, trying to imagine how he must look from a casual glance, from the periphery of that man with the umbrella and the briefcase passing by us with his coffee. Or how he must look to the younger versions of us, what they must have seen to call him before me.

He is now just rambling, talking, waiting for me to interrupt with forgiveness. I suppose I have that to offer, but only by way of mutual guilt.

"They called me too. I went on dates with them too."

"What? When?"

"Wednesday and Friday. Young me, then young you."

"I kind of wish you'd stop calling them that."

"You were the one who named them."

"I know. But as we go on it seems to muddle everything. Bryan says he doesn't see it." At this I have to think for a moment, realize that Bryan is the young him. There's a silence where Ben seems to do the math. "So I dated them first. I thought for sure it was the other way around. Got naked with Bryan and couldn't shake the idea that you'd already been all over him."

"You knew?"

"No. I suspected."

He had hoped. I could see it on his face, the smallest blush in his cheeks. He had hoped I had been with them first.

I guess this had been the central difference between Ben and I: he was always slightly jealous, while I was always slightly envious. Seeing me flirting with someone, he would be wracked with sadness. Seeing him flirting with someone, I would be excited, would want to see more. He runs his fingers through his hair, a mitt full, sits up, then slumps in his seat and sips his latte looking out at the water, nothing in him able to be still; envy itches him. He was looking for traces of me on them.

"So do you like one of them?" he asks me, fidgeting with his cup.

"I don't know." It's an honest answer.

His cellphone rings, he glances at it, pockets it again. I want to ask, want to know which one of them it was.

"And you? Do you like one of them?"

"Both. Maybe."

"Greedy."

"You asked."

"So you'll see them again?"

"Yes," his head lowers slightly, a tinge of guilt. Peculiar. "And you?" he asks looking up.

"I don't know." And I don't. Neither experience felt very real to me. Like each of the men was expecting me to be some version of me that I am not. Like someone had told them ahead of time how things should go.

"Yeah. I don't know which one I am interested in more. But yeah." And I feel the truth slither between my lungs and my stomach. Some part of me wants to compete. And, a child's hand outstretched to a tower of blocks, I want the rubble. Only part of me can recognize this and I file it away for later. As though there might be some reassurance in the aftermath that I foretold the impending calamity.

Just then I see the young versions of us, across the street walking down to the bay and the sea wall. Ben follows my gaze.

"You can't spy on them," I say.

"I know. I don't need to now. Do they look more happy or more unhappy?"

"I'm not sure. Which do you want them to be?"

"That's a little unfair."

"You asked."

"Yeah. I did," he looks at me, then back at them. "More happy . . . apart. Maybe," he squints, ignoring everything but the two men walking towards the bay.

"Do you think they know? Know that we were both with both of them?"

"That's a lot of knowing, "Ben says, intent on his latte and then taking a sip.

"Yes," I say. "A lot." And I mean for us more than them. It's a muddle.

"I should go," I say, taking one last sip of my coffee.

"Date tonight?" Ben asks, pretending to study the traffic outside, both of us silent at the elephant turd on the floor his simple question turned out to be.

"Thanks for the Americano," I add, standing.

And as I leave the café I note that judging by his phone ringing he's already heard from at least one of them. I've yet to hear from either.

My walk home, I find myself thinking of Ben, and how Ben must seem to the two of them, these younger versions of us. He has been working out. There is a clearer cut to his jaw, his cheekbones, and so his mouth seems fuller, begging for more kisses. His eyes have always been what I couldn't resist. He has his mother's eyes, a deep teak brown. They must see what only gradually unfolded to me. Along Denman Street, people in shops like aquariums, my reflection flashing between me and them as I wander down the street, glass walls cutting the day into boxes and I am on the wrong sides.

I decide to wait to see if they call. When the younger me does that afternoon, he's quiet and waiting on the other end of the phone for me to make the first move, suggest we see one another again, when and where. His waiting tires me.

The young Ben doesn't call. So I call him the next morning, Sunday. He was just going to call me. He seems to have no idea I've used that line before. Silence on my end provokes him to suggest "Wanna hang out?" which seems feeble to me. Then he suggests Thursday. Thursday, the weak choice. Wednesday would say he can't wait to see me, Friday would say that he's trying to make it something special, while Thursday is neither, the in between place that doesn't get in the way of two other possible options. I try not to roll my eyes on the other end of the phone.

One man is too easy and the other is too difficult. I need a Goldilocks option. Worse, I play the petulant child, not sure what I want, just certain I don't want Ben to end up with his younger self and for me to get the boring other me. I want them all, I want them all to want me, I don't want to be left alone without a place to sit in this peculiar musical chairs game of desire.

I realize then that what I want is to see these two men together. I am not even sure I want to be involved, just watching, free of the one's latches and the other's sprung windows. Seeing how they might look at each other, in these the last moments they'll be together. They won't last. They both know that. How will they kiss differently? What new and last minute kindnesses? What last drowning lurches to search out the other with mouth and hands, to remember every moment for later — part greediness, part abandon?

I want to see it. I want to be invisible and able to lean in close, notice the smaller details. Not who's on top or who makes the most noise, but the details never available to us, the lovers, the ones in the throes of it. I want to see the curl of an upper lip, the sweat forming in the smooth space behind an ear, the extra bend in the small of this one's back, as he reaches as far as muscle and bone will permit. That one's temple, swollen and desperate with pulse, the scent that gushes from one and the hitch in the breath of the other. The curl of the toes in his left foot where it cramps but he refuses to move and risk losing his grip on this slick, last hold. I will compose a thousand small maps and diagrams, capture each of these quickenings and twitches. I can't think of anything I want more than to see their last moments together. I want it even more, perhaps because I know they will not agree to this for me.

Ben meets me for dinner Sunday night, the lounge just past the crest of the hill. He seems suspicious that I've arranged for us to meet, bought our martinis already, a few sips ahead by the time he pulls out the chair and sits opposite me. I don't know how to begin.

"So now you're the mysterious one?"

I give half a nod. Try to find a way in. "So do you think both of them like you?"

"Yes, I guess they do."

"I guess, I mean do they desire you?"

"Yes." He seems discomfited, like he imagines he's cutting into my skin.

"Do you think they would be open to things you might suggest?"

"Yes, maybe."

He's searching my face now, enticed yet looking for the small print of what I am luring him into.

"I have something, something I want to try." I don't expect he's going to react well to this. While we were together he tried to get us to experiment several times, role play, he's the coach, I am the injured player, that kind of thing. Thing was, every attempt on his part seemed laced with fear that I was getting bored of our sex, fear that he would lose me if I got bored of our sex.

"I want to see the two of them together."

"Okay."

"But I am guessing that won't be likely, since they are breaking up."

"And . . . oh. Are you suggesting . . ."

"I'm guessing the only way they might be together is if they're with you."

"So you want to have sex, the four of us?"

"Not exactly. I want you to have sex with them, encourage them."

"And you want to watch."

"Just watch." I've stopped breathing. He seems to have stopped too. His jittery feet under the table, the table itself, the café, the street, the birds flying east for the night, all hang still in the thickness of this moment.

"Okay."

Breath returns in sips, then gushes in.

"I didn't think you'd agree."

"I didn't think I would either."

I want to ask why he agreed. But fear if he says it out loud he will change his mind.

"How will you ask them?"

He sips his martini, ponders.

"Ask each of them during sex," I suggest. "That way later when they remember the question they'll have a good association with the answer."

"Shit, wow. Did you ever do that to me?"

"No. Definitely not." I take a sip of my martini, the rim of the glass cracking a smirk on my lips.

He shakes his head, a smirk reply.

"Listen, I know it's weird, just —"

"No, don't explain it. I like not knowing. Maybe I'll ask later, maybe I'll want to know after. But not right now." Under the table his knees start to bounce again, the table slightly vibrating, the martinis rippling. "I just want to see what will happen."

His phone vibrates, he steals a glance down and, there, a warm crinkling in the corners of his eyes, an expression I haven't seen since other lifetimes, ones where he found me amusing. One of them has messaged him. He feels a warm crinkling.

I'm asking too much. I am asking him to take two men he has something with, two men who are falling out of love with one another or have fallen out of love already, and to convince them both to have sex with him while I watch. It's too much. But I won't say that. And he doesn't claim that in return. He seems resolved to make it happen. This will be the course of action. The way people go to the shore to watch the tidal wave, why they stand and watch the zeppelin burn, or play the video of towers falling over and over. I long for that crinkling, even if it means watching Ben crinkle for someone else.

Spaces between the spaces. I hanker, for all three of them really. I want to be in this mess of desire, yet I want thè precipice, the freedom of the hardwood floor, breath free from the entangling. Maybe I'll hang at the edge of the room, just watching. Maybe I will climb on the bed and embrace a sweet confusion of limbs. I can't tell.

He texts me Sunday. Two words: Wednesday night. Like colliding with a wall cheek first, I stop in the middle of the sidewalk reading the two words over and over. The end and the beginning all wrapped together.

Monday and Tuesday Ben maintains radio silence. All the details must fall away now, any chitchat, any clutter must be burned off in this short time so that we can get down to the bare vein of what will happen. We can't be the people we were before. We have to be just this. Four figures in a room.

And then it's Wednesday. We're meeting at their place. I requested this. The bed they once slept in, even though one of them now sleeps on the futon, the place where one had the right side to the other's left, the kitchen where they might have cooked together, or one cooked and the other did dishes. And the bathroom with their various products, symptoms of all their insecurities and flaws: hair thickening shampoo, acne medicine, teeth whitening strips, hemorrhoid cream. I might spend hours in the bathroom. There lie all the clues to the end and the beginning and the myriad ways they hid from one another and then

saw one another far too clearly. Can they already see what it will
be like, to have a bathroom with half of those symptoms? I could
tell them, how at first it seems simpler, how it seems cleaner,
more pure, and then soon after feels empty and sterile. The tiles
on Ben's floor must have seemed bare without my underwear
thrown there on the way into the shower. I imagine.

I arrive. They buzz me in. The apartment door is unlocked.
They are in the bedroom already. I nudge my sandals off at the
door, hear sounds of kisses and hands on skin from the bedroom. Against the back wall of the room, a wooden chair about
six feet from the three of them. My lungs billow, parachutes in
tree branches, breathless.

As I slide into the chair, a trickle of sweat runs between my
shoulder blades. I am startled by Ben's naked back, his ass. It's
been nine years since I have seen him naked. His muscles are
thicker all over, his waist less narrow, legs more solid, like his
body has settled into being a man. The other two I saw just last
week, but all three of them together seem much more naked. I
can't breathe. I might suffocate in the chair. Ben's back is to me.
He's kneeling on the bed, looking over his shoulder at me. They
both lie facing him, looking around him at me.

When he turns back to them, the other Ben sits up on his
knees and kisses him, a hand on each of his biceps. The younger
me shuffles closer on the bed, running his hands down the flanks
of his ex-boyfriend and I yearn to see his expression more closely.
The three of them aglow in the sparse room, flickered and washed
light from the candles in amongst the moving boxes. They are
ugly, too, pale and vulnerable and contorting. Sublime and dis-
gusting, I suffocate between the three of them, my mouth wet,
my chest caught on the edge of a heave of weeping. Languor and
tremble, they are limb lost, bare to me like bodies thrown up on
a beach, buffeted by each other in waves.

Sex wasn't like this with Ben and me. At least not at the end. What was the measure of my numbness? The very last time we were together, I didn't want to have sex. I hardly recognized Ben in those last days, pinballing around the apartment, leaving late at night, sometimes not coming back, door clicking unlocked and him filling rooms shiny new and Teflon. I couldn't be in the same room without feeling a wound coming on. I was pretending to be napping on the futon that afternoon. June, I think. Swelter and breezeless, the sheet cloying to my bare back and legs. He slid in behind me. I couldn't move. Paralysis and fatigue. What could he possibly want in these last staggering days? And yet I couldn't refuse him. I let him move his hands over me, let him run his mouth down my shoulder blades, my spine. He ran his hands down me, rubbed me, I was headless. Ceasing to be with each nuzzle, each press.

Finished. He pulled the sheet loosely back over me. He said goodbye. I didn't. I wonder how he remembers all this. The young Ben is kissing my Ben. Pushing him back down on the bed while young me runs his hand up Ben's chest.

In that moment I move from wanting to be in among them, pressed to the quick, to now wanting to flee, to forget we ever met them, forget I ever saw Ben naked again.

Maybe some part of me thought I could catch a glimpse of what we went through in those last days. Maybe. Though now I remember mostly numbness, one long humid, airless night, the tide withdrawn from bare sand and a barrage of crabs and night birds. A thick pointless waiting.

Tonight, instead of the naked, fervent tableau, the current of bodies crashing under bodies, a diorama of last longings, I sit on a wooden chair watching the feckless scurrying of animals in the branches of cherry trees. I want them to be done. Want them to get off. I want to slip from the room, to the hallway, to the elevator, to the lobby, to the street, to —

Where does one go after this?

That's when I catch Ben looking at me. It's the briefest moment. Like he's making sure I am still there. And I am in the vice
grips again, against the roof of his clenched mouth, in the breathless, still water waiting to rise or float down through the seaweed
fronds.

I seek to taste their last days, then get tangled in the sheets.
I still don't see how this ends, but I can feel these small pulses
of other possible beginnings. Some taste like the one who looks
like me, his caramel tanned neck, and others thrum like him,
that other Ben with the rush to forget hands. I give a small blink
of a nod. One Ben can see. So he turns back to the two of them.
And because that nod makes him not worry, he doesn't hear the
door close.

It's late. The street thrums with people pressing up against
the glass of the gelaterias. From the dusty sidewalks, I watch the
people watchers in café windows, then wash with the sleepless
crowd down towards the water, a few waiters shifting on their
feet, checking on phones for messages that don't arrive, waiting
for the last diners to leave. A Ben at a metal table outside a pizza-
by-the-slice place picks pepperoni slices off his pizza, licks his
fingers. Another Ben in the convenience store uncharacteristic-
ally buys lottery tickets. And even a Ben and a me on a gelato
date, a little more beardy and chubby, using little plastic spoons
to try each other's flavours, more intent on tastes than the date.
I cross the street and stop on the seawall looking over the beach,
the walkers in the dark. Down at the water line, the waves rinse
and repeat their ablutions, shushing the murmurs of the birds
and squirrels now sleeping in the trees.

## ACKNOWLEDGMENTS

"Blink" appeared in *The Fiddlehead* 256 (Summer 2013).
"Mirrorball" appeared in *Pank Magazine* 6.13 "Queer Two."
"Beautifully Useless" appeared in *Ryga* 7.

This book was completed with the support of The Canada Council for the Arts.

"You alone can do it, but you can't do it alone" the proverb goes, and though it seems to be mostly employed in reference to a higher power, I am co-opting it here to pay tribute to the extraordinary people who I am blessed to have in my life and who helped make this book possible.

My deepest gratitude to Suzette Mayr who signed on to work as editor with me again for this book. I am in awe of her thorough, thoughtful, and supportive feedback. I can't say enough about what a gift she is as an editor. Also thanks to the crew at NeWest Press, Paul, Matt, Tiiu, and the wonderful designer Natalie Olsen.

I am indebted to several trusted readers: Rachel Warburton, Augie Westhaver, Douglas Ferguson, Douglas Glover, Eden Robinson, Susan Goldberg, Mary Chapman, Allison Mack, Kate Sutherland, Judith Leggatt, and Mark Anthony Jarman. Of these, foremost, the incredible Sophie Lavoie who has read more of my words than anyone and even translated some of them into other languages.

My deepest gratitude for the ones who I message and who message me when the writing air gets thin and the ground gets shaky: Ward Bingham, Mary Chapman, Allison Mack, Douglas Glover in particular.

And for all my friends who understand and support why I am such a bore and off on my own much of the time. Thanks for the Dance Dance Revolutions, the foods, the beverages, and for dragging me out of the tower and making me let my hair down.

I have an incredible family spread over the country, from Thunder Bay, to British Columbia, to the east coast, who are immensely supportive. They are also a rich source of story material. This book would not exist without both those things.

My life and writing life are a bit of a gypsy existence, so thanks to Jones Henry, Tom Fedechko, Ward Bingham, Trevor Davidson, Allison Mack, Jason Madore, for always being so lovely as to offer me homes in other places.

A special thanks to the extraordinary people at Executive Success Programs who have helped me to push and develop myself as a human being and an artist: Allison Mack, Megan Mumford, John Fox, Marc Elliot, Ken Kozak, Lauren Salzman, Sarah Edmondson, Mark Vicente, Wendy Rosen-Brooks, and most foundationally Keith Raniere and Nancy Salzman. Without these people there would have been more video games played, fewer stories written. Thanks for teaching me deeper compassion and expression.

A huge thanks to the Department of English at the University of New Brunswick, the staff, my colleagues, and my students. I get to work in a place that passionately cares about stories. For that I am eternally grateful.

**R.W. GRAY**'s poetry and prose have appeared in numerous journals and anthologies. His first collection of short stories, *Crisp,* was published by NeWest Press. An award-winning filmmaker and screenwriter, he has had over ten short films produced. He lives in Fredericton, where he is a professor of film and screenwriting in the English Department at the University of New Brunswick.

¶ This book was typeset in FF Tundra, a serif with particularly narrow letterforms created by Ludwig Übele with an emphasis on horizontal movement. The accompanying sans serif is Knockout designed by Hoefler & Co.